AfterStrike

(An Unforgettable Thriller)

By L.J. Sellers

AfterStrike
Copyright © 2023 by L.J. Sellers

Cover art by Gwen Rhoads

ISBN: 978-1-7345418-7-8
Published in the USA by Spellbinder Press

Chapter 1

The Turbulent Present
Abandoned and alone

Sept. 7, Wilsonville, OR

Remi opened her eyes, her fists clenched. "It's still not coming back."

Her counselor sighed. "I'm sorry. That's the only method I know for recalling memories. I think it's time to see a specialist, someone who can help you in a more neurologic way." The woman's robust voice didn't match her thin, aging body.

"You're dumping me?" Another unexpected blow. Remi had found Joanne's name in her phone contacts and assumed they had a history. Even though this musty, low-rent office didn't give off a professional vibe, she'd counted on this woman to help get her life back.

"Please don't see it that way." Joanne scooted forward, her eyes troubled. "This situation is complex for me. During our earlier sessions, before the incident, you told me things about your past, about your guilt. Now that you can't remember any of that, it would be unethical and probably counterproductive for me to remind you. So I shouldn't see you until you've recovered." The counselor reached for a notepad. "I'll refer you to a neuropsychologist in Portland."

Remi shook her head. "I can't start over. It's all been too much." She'd had a sliver of hope when she'd walked in, but now she felt abandoned and alone. *That would be the tagline on her gravestone.*

"I'm still available by phone if you have destructive impulses and need to talk." Joanne held out the referral note.

Remi let out a harsh laugh. *Destructive impulses* would be her footnote. "I'll be fine. Thanks though."

She bolted from the office, knowing she would never be back. Coming here the first time a year ago had felt like cracking open her own chest. She remembered the pain of that first session if not the details. Then two months earlier—just as she was able to get through a day without hating herself—she'd suffered *the strike* and woken up with unbearable pain and no memory. Pieces of her recent life in this town had come back, but the rest of her past was still a total blank.

What was the point of seeing yet another specialist? So they could tell her she was physically fine and to *just be patient?* The doctor who'd treated her in the ER kept saying that, and his indifference, especially to her physical distress, infuriated her. Remi reached for her phone to delete the counselor's contact, but she'd left the cell in her car.

At the bottom of the exterior stairs, she swore. Not only was it drizzling—signaling summer's coming end—some jackass had parked his crappy van too close to her Mazda. Now she would have to squeeze her wide hips in sideways like a contortionist. She shuffled across the secluded back lot, wincing at the literal pain in her ass and wishing she'd dressed warmer. As she grabbed the driver's side handle, a flash of panic. *Where was Tuck?*

Behind her, the van's sliding door clanged open. Instinctual fear made her spin around to run, but she was too slow. A powerful hand pressed a vile rag against her mouth and a massive arm wrapped around her rib cage. With a quick lift, the man heaved her like a sack of cement. From inside the van, someone grabbed her armpits and pulled her into the dark space.

"Motherfu—" She couldn't form the rest of the word. Her tongue wouldn't work and her brain felt woozy. Yet before she blacked out, a vague thought came together. *Whoever she'd been hiding from had finally found her.*

Chapter 2

The Recent Past
Did you call me Remi?

July 3, two months earlier

Thunder boomed in the dark sky and Remi tensed. A storm hadn't been in the forecast, so the sky-shaking noise caught her off guard. Every fiber in her body wanted to bolt for the building, but she had to round up the kids first. She ran toward the girls on the swing set. "Go inside!" She pointed at the back door. "Now!"

Remi pivoted toward the boys playing basketball and repeated her frantic message. Three of the kids went wide-eyed and followed the girls, but Trevor, a hyper five-year old, took another run at the low hoop. Panic made her heart pound in her ears. "I said now!"

The boy turned, shocked at her tone, but instead of running toward the daycare, he burst into tears and bolted to the corner of the fenced-in play area.

Shit. She didn't have time for this.

The sky flashed, a light so bright it hurt her eyes.

"Get inside!" Remi dashed toward him, but he dodged her. Cursing loudly, she gave chase, catching him as he rounded the

4

big metal slide. She scooped him up and tried to run, but he was heavy and kicked at her knees. Thunder boomed again, and her lungs fought for air against her tight chest. *Almost there.* As she reached the patio, the boy squirmed out of her arms and scurried in the door ahead of her.

A moment later, the air sizzled and a bolt of lightning knocked her to the ground. The pain was so intense Remi blacked out before her face hit the concrete.

She woke to the sound of concerned voices, a man and a woman talking softly nearby. Her eyes fought to stay closed like they did sometimes on sleepy mornings, but she managed to force a word out of her parched mouth. "Water." Why did she hurt everywhere?

One voice came closer. "Remi, can you hear me? I see you blinking."

Who was Remi? "Water." She forced her eyes open.

The man, who seemed young and dressed in white, was rather blurry as he leaned in and offered a straw. The cool liquid soothed her mouth, and the room came into focus: a small exam space in the back of an ER.

"Why am I here?" Dread filled her chest as she realized she couldn't remember what had happened.

"You were hit by lightning at the daycare."

What? Confused, she sat up and peeked under the sheet. Her body had nice breasts that were starting to sag and a layer of pudge on her belly. How could she not remember this? Panic rolled in like a tidal surge, threatening to drown her.

"You should lay back and rest." The man pressed a lever to raise the top of the wheeled bed. "I'm Dr. Azul Sanjay."

"Did you call me Remi?"

A flash of concern. "Your work badge says Remi Bartel."

She gulped for breath. "I can't remember anything."

"We'll get you a CT scan and see what's happening." The doctor sounded calm, but his eyes were uncertain. "Your memory loss is likely temporary." An uncomfortable pause. "I've never treated a high-voltage shock patient, but my understanding is that the effects are short-term."

"Good to hear. Because I need to get home." Remi didn't know why, but the feeling was urgent. "How long have I been here?"

"Two hours or so."

Remi glanced at the wall clock: *3:45. About the time she usually got home from work.* The thought floated in and out, untethered to specific details. Still, it offered hope her memory would return.

Dr. Sanjay shifted. "You don't seem to have any injuries except for the burns where the lightning entered and exited your body. As soon as you feel ready, we can release you."

Remi touched the white bandage taped to her right shoulder socket. Where was the other burn? She started to ask, then realized she knew. The searing pain in her left butt cheek now made sense. "Have you given me any pain medication?"

"No. I wanted to see how you felt first."

"Like I've been dunked in a deep fryer with a vice-clamp around my head, then branded on the ass." She tried to smile. "So put some of the good stuff in my IV, please."

The doctor looked surprised. "On a scale of one to ten, with ten being the worst pain you can imagine, what's your level?"

"I thought I just told you, but I'll say eight or nine, just to be clear."

A long moment of silence. "Okay. We'll get some anti-inflammatory in your line, and I'll write you a script for ten Percocet with no refills."

"Thanks. I'd like to leave soon." *And go where?* Remi tried to visualize her home. A small brown cottage came to mind. *No.* That was her childhood home. "Where are we, by the way?"

"Wilsonville."

It meant nothing to her. "Can you be more specific?"

"It's a small town south of Portland, Oregon."

The west coast seemed familiar and correct. Time to get out there and see it. Maybe the visual images would trigger actual memories. "Where's my purse? With my driver's license?"

"It's likely still at the daycare. We'll call them. Anyone else we should contact? A spouse? Family?"

Remi couldn't think of a single person she might know. "After the CT scan, will you call an Uber for me?" Being alone with the pain and memory loss rather terrified her, but lying in this windowless room not knowing anything felt like a layer of hell Dante hadn't experienced.

Chapter 3

The Recent Past

Her life had once been more vibrant

A few hours later

Remi walked into KinderCare, blinking at the bright colors. If she worked here, she must like kids, but she didn't remember this place. Or anything else. Her CT scan hadn't shown an injury to her skull or brain, but her mind seemed to be lost in a thick fog. The sensation was bizarre and embarrassing and she wanted to get this interaction over quickly. Her headache had eased, but so had the effect of the anti-inflammatory, and her burns hurt with every movement.

"Remi!" The stout woman behind the counter desk beamed. "I'm so glad you're okay. We've all been worried sick."

Remi tried to be pleasant. "Thanks." She glanced at the receptionist's badge. "Cheri."

"You're wearing hospital scrubs. Are you sure—?"

"I'm fine. My clothes were burned and they cut them off me."

"Oh right." Cheri stood. "Let me get the rest of the staff. They'll want to—"

"No. Please. I'm not up for it. I just need my purse."

"Of course." Cheri reached under the counter and held out a brown canvas shoulder bag.

Remi took it, dug around for a wallet, then stared at her driver's license. The woman in the photo looked vaguely familiar: thirty-five or so with ash-blonde hair, hazel eyes, and round cheeks. Kinda pretty, but not really. The name read: *Remi Lynn Bartel.* She noted the date of birth and realized she was only thirty-one. She looked up at Cheri. "My memory is fuzzy. Do I have a car here?"

The receptionist frowned. "The green Mazda."

"Thanks. I need to go."

"Are you sure you should be alone?"

"I'm not sure of anything, except that I need to get home." Remi also remembered the address on her license after glancing at it only briefly. That struck her as odd.

From an interior door, a young boy burst into the lobby. "Remi!" He threw his arms around her legs. "I'm so sorry you were hurt."

Startled by his affection and concern, Remi patted his head. "Thanks. I think I'll be okay." She felt bad about not remembering his name.

He looked up. "Jason told me you were dead."

Remi chuckled and stepped back. "Do I look like a zombie?" She forced a smile. "I was just asleep for a while. Now I have to go home and rest."

"You'll be back tomorrow?"

"Maybe not 'til next week. Bye for now." She hurried out before anyone else confronted her.

In the car, which was impressively clean, she gave Google Maps her address and let its nagging voice guide her. As she drove through Wilsonville, the sign for *Boonsferry Landing* amused her, and directions to *Coffee Lake* made her smile. Had she grown up in this funky little town or purposely moved here? When the Nag told her she'd arrived, Remi stopped at the end of a short side street and stared at the two-story farmhouse. *This wasn't it.* She noticed two mailboxes, then realized the driveway went past the house to another dwelling in back. Remi eased down the cracked, narrow concrete, spotted a cute cottage, and felt a little less intimidated. On the porch, a planter bloomed with purple petunias. Had she planted them? She stepped up to the door and panic hit her. What if she had a roommate or boyfriend inside? Would she even know their name?

Remi unlocked the door with the other key on her set and stepped inside. The air smelled of fried onions, a strangely comforting scent. Something banged in the back of the house, startling her. Rapid clicking sounds, then a little white dog with a brown face burst across the room. He leapt into her arms, wiggling and kissing her face.

"Tuck!"

Love surged in her heart, overwhelming her to the point of tears. She wasn't alone. This little guy was her life—and remembering his name delighted her. She squeezed him tight, then sat on the bench by the door, letting him jump and rub all over her until he settled down. By then, pain screamed at her to get up, and she took one of the Percocets she'd picked up at the hospital pharmacy. She needed to put something in her stomach soon, or the oxy might make her nauseous, but she wanted to explore the house first.

The tour took all of three minutes, with Tuck padding along. In addition to the boxy living room and galley kitchen, she had two small bedrooms, a hall bath with outdated fixtures, and a closet-sized laundry room with a dog door leading outside. The main bedroom was tidy and simple, the only color a mint-green blanket, the only decoration a vase with dried flowers on the dresser. The simplicity suited her, yet also made her sad, as though her life had once been more vibrant.

"Not much to look at, huh, Tuck?"

He wagged his tail, and they wandered back down the hall. The spare room contained a narrow desk with a laptop, a dust-covered stationary bike, and a stack of empty retail boxes. They'd once contained a flat-screen TV, an electric can opener, and sets of plates, bowls, and glasses. She'd either recently purchased these things, or she never threw away boxes.

A memory tickled her subconscious, like the way her nose itched before a sneeze. Exhausted, Remi headed back to the kitchen. She needed to eat, take some aspirin, and rest for a while.

Halfway through a bowl of canned chili, with Tuck eating his share nearby, an image surfaced. She was stepping out of her car at a park, where she'd looked around and liked what she saw—a quaint, lush-green town where she could feel safe. Her backseat had some luggage, a blanket, and a bag of dog food. Tuck, of course, was at her side.

When had she moved to this place? By the look of the house, particularly the retail boxes, maybe only a few months ago. Yet she knew it had been longer, and she'd come here for a reason. Someone to be close to? *No.* Fear squeezed her heart. Someone to get away from… in yet another life she couldn't remember.

Not wanting to think about it, Remi pulled out her cellphone. Only four contacts were listed: *Izzy, landlord; Cheri, KinderCare; Joanne, counselor; and Chris.* No label. Was he, or she, a friend? Remi hoped so. But she would wait for her memory to return before calling. Not knowing anything about herself, or her friends, was humiliating.

"The memory loss is likely temporary. I've never treated a high-voltage shock patient, but my understanding is that the effects are short-term."

She recalled every word, including the doctor's hesitation to admit he'd never treated an electrical burn. Relief washed over her. At least her ability to remember new things was fine, even better than she would've expected.

She finished her chili, rinsed their bowls, then moved to the cozy recliner in the minimalist living room. Tuck jumped into her lap and she stroked his head. "My sweet boy. I'm so glad I have you." Remi closed her eyes. Her memories would come back, her body would heal, and she would be okay. She had to believe that.

Chapter 4

The Turbulent Present

Debts must be paid

Sept. 7, on the road (shortly after the kidnapping)

Remi opened her eyes, but darkness still engulfed her. Had she gone blind? Her heart fluttered and she tried to sit up, then realized she wasn't in bed. Movement, traffic sounds, and a hard metal floor made her realize she was in the cargo bay of a van. In a rush, she recalled the strong hands in the parking lot and the chloroform rag. *Oh fuck.* She'd been kidnapped. She tried again to move, but her wrists and ankles were bound and she had a cloth bag over her head. Panic flooded her chest and caught in her throat. Where were they going? To a forest to rape and kill her? *No. Don't catastrophize the future. Just stay in the moment.* Remi focused on what she could hear.

Heavy breathing only a few feet away.

A moment later, the driver muttered something about "takin' the 205."

They were headed north, toward Portland. "What's happening?" she called out. Or at least that's what she tried to say, but the tape over her mouth garbled the words.

"Shut up." Thick fingers squeezed her face, pressing the canvas into her tender skin.

Another wave of panic. Where was Tuck? Had they killed him to keep him quiet? "What about my dog?" Remi shouted, unable to control her fear.

A fist slammed into her gut. Unable to see it coming, she hadn't braced and the blow knocked the wind out of her. She couldn't suck in more oxygen because of the tape on her mouth and the bag over her head. Her mind clouded and she blacked out again.

When she woke, she stayed quiet, listening for any sound of Tuck. But she heard only the hum of freeway traffic and men breathing. *Please don't let doggo be dead.* The thought crushed her and warm tears pooled in her eyes. Maybe they'd simply opened her car door and let him go. But Tuck wasn't a runner. He might've explored the area, but he would have come back to the car to wait for her. The poor little guy didn't deserve whatever was happening.

Did she? Remi had no idea. Her life before Wilsonville was still a blank, but she had to assume she'd pissed off these nasty people. Queasy dread filled her belly. This was a punishment, and it wasn't over.

The van slowed, and a turn signal started to click. They were exiting the freeway. Remi tried to calculate how far they'd traveled, but she had no idea how long she'd been unconscious either time. Within a few minutes, she sensed they were in a densely populated area with frequent stoplights. Portland? Or had they crossed the river into Vancouver? After several more turns, they made a slow left, then soon rolled to a stop.

"I'm cutting your feet loose so you can walk." A gruff voice, probably the big guy. "Don't do anything stupid or your dog will suffer."

Tuck was alive!

The man grabbed her ankles, dragged her out the side door, and jerked her to her feet. "You take her, Seth," he called to the driver.

Remi pulled in a deep breath. Despite the blindfold, she knew she was in a garage. The scent of damp concrete and metal tools was intense and familiar.

Big Guy yanked off her mask and she saw him for the first time. Bald, with a beard and neck tattoos—the hillbilly-thug look so popular with guys her age. He pushed aside his unzipped jacket and displayed a dark handgun tucked into his jeans.

At least a bullet to her head would be quick.

The thug reached into the back of the van and came out with a wire pet cage. Inside, Tuck lay still.

Doggo had been drugged! But he looked unharmed. Remi breathed a sigh of relief.

Big Guy walked away, and the driver, a gaunt man with unwashed hair and a meth-scab face, grabbed her arm. "Let's go." As Seth led her across the garage, Remi glanced around for a weapon. Lawnmower, gas cans, an old bike. The only potential item was an axe hooked on a wall peg. But her wrists were still bound with a zip-tie, so she needed something small and easy to manage. They stepped into a kitchen and she scanned the counters for a knife holder. There, next to the microwave.

If she could grab one and stab Seth in the neck...

"Hey, Blake, where do you want her?" Seth called across the house.

"Put her in the dining room," Blake yelled back. "We don't want blood on the carpet. This is an Airbnb rental."

Remi's gut roiled. They were gonna torture her?

A minute later, Blake met them at the table, a sturdy wood piece that he pushed against the wall like it was made of foam. He pulled a chair into the cleared spaced, shoved Remi down onto it, and ripped the tape off her mouth.

Fear made her reckless and she shouted, "What the hell is this about?"

Big Guy backhanded her across the face. "Never raise your voice to me."

Cheek and mouth stinging, Remi tasted blood. In the back of the house, Tuck barked, a muted sound.

Remi forced herself to sound polite. "I just want to know what's going on. And why you have my dog."

Her captor grinned. "He's my leverage. If you do your part, he'll be fine. If not, I'll kill him slowly right in front of you."

Motherfucker! "What part? What do you want from me?"

"We need you to listen to a conversation and report back what they say."

A strange request, but it seemed easy enough. "Then you'll let me go?"

Blake laughed. "It's not up to me, but if the payoff is big enough, Yano might consider it."

"Who's Yano?"

"You really don't remember?" He pulled up a chair and sat across from her. "That lightning really messed up your brain, huh?"

"Yeah."

"But that doesn't change the past, and you owe big debts that must be paid. Yano is still nail-spitting mad at you."

What had she done? "I'll pay those debts if I can. There's no need to hurt me or Tuck."

A wicked smile this time. "Not yet anyway." Blake turned to his partner. "Get some ice for her face. She needs to look good for her gig tomorrow."

The skinny guy hurried toward the fridge.

"What gig?" Remi asked.

"You'll be a waitress at a small private dinner. I have you set up with the service, and you'll fill in for another girl at the last minute."

"I don't think I have those skills." Remi hated the tremor in her voice.

"Sure you do. You were serving cocktails at the Silverstone when Yano first spotted you."

How could she not remember a job like that?

Blake shook his head with a disappointed expression. "You looked a lot better back then. Blonder, skinnier"—he gestured at her face—"prettier. But I see now that was mostly makeup."

She wanted to give him both middle fingers, but resisted. Seth came back with a cold gel-pack and held it to her sore face for a minute.

When he stepped away, Remi asked, "What conversation am I supposed to listen to?"

"The only three men in the room. And they're gonna talk about legislation and stock trades, like always."

A politician with stock traders; no surprise there. But Yano and this revenge-kidnap thing had bigger connections than she would have guessed. Which could be bad news for her. But then again, maybe she could escape during the server gig, or alert someone to her situation. But the thugs had Tuck. Could she walk away from him to save herself?

Never!

"I'll help if I can, but you have to let me see my dog. I need to know he's okay."

"You saw him, and he's just dandy," Blake snarled. "But in case you decide to risk your dog's life, we're keeping tabs on your mother too."

A mental image came into focus: A slender woman with dark hair pulled back into a tight bun and a serious expression. The visual disappeared just as quickly, leaving Remi with mixed emotions—longing, resentment, and a sense she hadn't been close to the woman in a long time. She'd wondered about her family since the lightning strike, but she had nothing: no memories, no photos, no phone numbers. That was obviously for the best, considering the danger she could put them in.

"I don't remember my mother, but leave her alone. I'll do what you want." Remi shifted in the hard chair. She had nothing left to lose—except a one-eyed dog who was probably scared and peeing all over his crate. "Can I please see Tuck? He'll behave better if he knows I'm okay."

Blake got up and headed for the hall, and Seth applied the cold gel pack again. When Big Guy came back, he carried the cage with Tuck inside. Doggo was on his feet and staring at her, but his eye was cloudy.

"Did you drug him?"

"A little. I can't have him barkin' for days."

Days? Remi swallowed hard. "Where is the dinner I'm supposed to serve?"

"That doesn't matter."

None of this made sense. "Why do you need me? Why not just send in someone with a recorder?"

"You'll see."

Another wave of dread. "Why me?"

"That news story said you had super memory skills for anything you read or heard, and we need to know every word."

Oh shit. That was how they'd found her. Remi hung her head. She should have never gone to those meetings.

Chapter 5

The Recent Past

You're in some shit, aren't ya?

July 6, Wilsonville (day 3 after the strike)

Remi woke to the sound of knocking, followed by short barks. Tuck was already on the move as she struggled to get up from the recliner. *Please let this pain be temporary.* She shuffled toward the door, and even with closed curtains, she could tell it was almost dark.

"Who is it?"

"Izzy. Sorry to bug you, but your rent is overdue."

Questions flooded her foggy brain, but Remi recalled Izzy's name from her cell phone with the label *landlord*. Maybe Izzy lived in the farmhouse out front. Remi opened the door. The woman, mid-fifties with a curly gray afro, bent over and petted Tuck, who seemed happy for the attention.

A good sign. "Sorry I'm late with the rent. I've had a bad week."

Izzy squinted. "No problem. What happened? You look kinda spacey."

"Yeah. I got hit by lightning."

"Jumpin' Jesus." Izzy shook her head. "That musta hurt."

"It burned me going in and out." Remi had hoped to hide

her bigger issue, but in this moment of pain and confusion, she needed help. If Tuck trusted Izzy, she would too. "I also lost my memory, so I don't even know how much my rent is, let alone, how to pay it."

"Wow, girl. You're in some shit, aren't ya?"

"A big, sloppy pile of it."

Izzy chuckled, and Remi did too. "What do I owe you?"

"Fifteen-hundred. And you always pay in cash."

The rent seemed a bit much, but Remi had a gut feeling the cash-only request was hers. "Let me look around, and I'll get back to you."

"Tomorrow morning is fine. You takin' a few days off?"

Remi let out another painful laugh. "Or maybe a year."

"That bad, huh?" Izzy laid a hand on her arm. "Can I bring you something to eat? I've got some leftover soup."

"Sounds good. My fridge is down to a chunk of cheese and two apples."

"You don't cook, do ya?"

"I don't know." Based on her cupboard full of canned chili, which she was sick of, probably not. "Can I ask a weird question?"

"Lay it on me."

"Do we have a rental contract? I don't even know when I moved here."

"Goin' on two years now. You paid a big deposit to avoid any paperwork." Izzy gestured at a powerline leading to Remi's cottage. "Your utilities are in my name, so the rent money covers those too."

"Perfect. I'll get the cash to you soon." *If she had any and could locate it.*

Izzy petted Tuck again, then waved and walked away.

Remi shuffled to the kitchen and opened her prescription bottle. Three pain pills left. *Shit.* That wasn't enough. Her pain wasn't going anywhere. She swallowed one and hoped to save the others for emergency use only.

After putting a kettle on the stove for tea, she started pulling open drawers. She might have already taken her rent money out of the bank, but even if she hadn't, she needed to find a checkbook or some way of identifying the bank. Any other information that would help her figure out who the hell lived here would be nice too.

No checkbook. But she was surprised to discover many of her drawers were half empty, including the *junk* drawer on the end of the counter. Had she always been a minimalist?

Remi headed for her bedroom to search, and Tuck followed with his usual excited expectation. She searched her dresser for the first time and found those drawers sparsely packed as well. The nightstand had nothing except an e-reader tablet. Reaching to push aside clothes hanging in her closet hurt her armpit burn, but she only had two sun dresses, four long-sleeved shirts, and a jacket, so it didn't take long. The lack of paperwork anywhere frustrated her. She needed information!

She pulled a small suitcase out of the closet and spotted a blanket wadded on the floor. *Weird.* She knelt down, wincing at the pain, and lifted the blanket. Under it sat a metallic-gray safe about twenty inches tall, including the wheels.

"Well, well." Maybe this was where she kept important things.

She pulled the safe forward into the light of the room and stared at the combination lock. No numbers came to mind. A smart person wouldn't use their birthday—too easy for someone else to guess—but picking four random numbers didn't seem like something she would do.

"Well, Tuck, this could be a problem."

He waged his tail and licked her hand.

A vague image of an alphabet code flashed in Remi's mind. She went to the desk and turned on the laptop, a cheap Chromebook. She had no memory of buying or using it, but operating on muscle memory, she opened a browser and googled *alphabet number* code. She clicked the first link and a two-column chart displayed. She tried her name first: R/18, E/5, M/13, I/9. That didn't work, so she tried it spelled backward. *Nope.* What next? The name or number had to be significant, but clever. Remi smiled and tried Tuck's name. When it didn't work, she got worried, but then used the numbers backward.

The lock clicked, and she pulled open the thick metal door.

Holy shit!

Compact stacks of cash filled most of the safe, with a few small bundles in front. Where had all this come from?

Chapter 6

The Recent Past
She looked like a freak

Moments later

S he scooped the stacks out to the floor and started counting. Twenty-six thousand, three-hundred and seventy-five dollars. What kind of person kept that much in a safe? Someone who didn't trust banks, wasn't supposed to have the cash, or didn't want to pay taxes on it. Or maybe she was all three. Yet, none of those personalities seemed right. Also, it wasn't that much money. A nice savings, but it would disappear fast if she didn't go back to work soon.

She shoved her hand to the back of the safe and rummaged around, hoping to find some paperwork. But there was nothing. No birth certificate, no bank statements. She'd found the title to her car earlier in the glove box, but it hadn't provided any new information. As she pulled her hand back out, her fingers brushed against something flat and metal. Remi picked it up.

A key.

To what? Maybe a safe deposit box, where she kept important papers. Possibly more cash. But where the hell was the box?

Her foggy brain had no idea. She fought back tears. This was so fucked up.

After dinner that evening, unable to bear the anguish, Remi took her last oxy. She'd rationed the ten pills the doc had allowed, but only by spending most of her time resting or sleeping. Who the hell wanted to live that way? She also couldn't stand the feel of her own skin any longer. Time to take a shower. She had soaped her stinky parts with a washrag, but the doctor had said not to get her burns wet for a day or so.

In the bathroom, she removed her sleeveless jersey, cringing as she lifted her arms. Gently, she pulled the tape from the nook of her pit, then removed the bandage.

Holy fuck! The burn's center had started to blacken and pucker like a piece of fire-pit wood. If that weren't ugly enough, a crazy pattern of spindly red scars extended down her side to join the wound on her ass. Remi stared, open-mouthed, at the carnage. She looked like a freak.

Please don't let it be permanent.

Finally, she tore her eyes away long enough to remove the lower bandage, then took a moment to examine the rest of her body. No C-section or hysterectomy scars. A wave of sadness hit her. What if she had a kid somewhere? A baby she'd abandoned or given up for adoption. *No.* She could never forget someone so important.

She lifted a leg to the counter and spotted a white scar running down her thigh. Too weird and ragged for a surgery, so probably an earlier injury. From what though? Climbing over a barb-wire fence? Remi checked her other leg, then pivoted to see more of her backside. For the first time, she noticed a pink, roundish scar behind her right shoulder. No clue what happened there. But she wasn't surprised to discover she was accident prone. She'd tripped and fallen twice while limping around the house.

In the shower, she savored the joy of warm water gushing over her battered body. Ashamed she'd waited this long to get fully clean, Remi vowed to stop napping and watching TV, ignore the pain, and get on with her life. Not only was she bored and restless, the few flashes of memory she'd recovered—all about being in this house—had happened when she was moving around. Something had to give.

Chapter 7

The Recent Past
It sounded shady, but she didn't care

July 7 (day 4 after the strike)

Remi woke with the same headache she did every morning. Pushing through the pain and mental fog, she struggled to get out of bed. Tuck hit the floor with his usual enthusiasm.

"Showoff."

As he headed for his dog door to the backyard, she shuffled into the bathroom and pulled off her bandages. It was time to start letting her burns dry out for periods of time, no matter how bad it felt. She set a goal of three hours. When the pain became unbearable, she would apply ointment and re-cover them. She planned to walk more as well, despite how much it hurt. Her already pudgy body seemed to be expanding. Thank god, there wasn't a scale in the house. Seeing the number would be a kick in the teeth, and she was already depressed.

For a full minute, she stared at the red spindly scars on her side. They seemed even more vivid this morning. Maybe she could find a cream that would help them fade. *Stop looking!* Remi pulled her comfy jersey back on, then trudged up the hall, wincing at the rhythmic pain of her rolling glutes.

Twelve hours without meds.

In the kitchen, she filled Tuck's bowl, then made herself black tea and cinnamon toast, the same thing she'd eaten the last few mornings. With her one good butt cheek on the counter stool, she carefully cut off the crust. Tuck trotted up and sat to wait for the discards. As she bent over to offer him a bite, a sharp memory surfaced. She had tripped over the dog one morning and landed sprawled on her belly. She remembered laughing and wishing she had a recording to send to Funniest Home Videos. The recall was encouraging, but in the moment, it was all she could do to smile at her poor baby. Tuck knew she wasn't herself and seemed confused and sad.

After she put her plate in the sink, she called the main number on the hospital paperwork. "This is Remi Bartel. I need to speak with Dr. Sanjay."

"He's not on call in the ER today." The woman sounded rushed and ready to hang up.

"Can someone else help me? I'm still in a lot of pain and I need a prescription refill."

"Spell your name, please."

After some back-and-forth about who she was and when she'd visited the ER, the clinic worker said, "You need a follow-up visit with Dr. Sanjay. His number should be on your discharge papers."

"Where? I didn't see it."

"It's on the back page with all his details."

"Thanks." Remi scanned the pages she'd never read, found another number, and made a second call. After setting up an appointment for the next week, she asked about getting a refill.

"You'll have to wait until you see the doctor." The faceless voice might as well have been a robot.

"But I'm in horrible pain now. I mean all the time."

"I'm sorry. Have you tried using ice?"

Fuck that. "Lightning came out of my butt cheek. It hurts just to walk down the hall."

"I'll talk to the doctor, but I know he'll want to see you."

"I'll text him a picture." Remi ended the call and bellowed in frustration. Tuck whimpered nearby, and she resisted the urge to smash her phone on the counter. When had the medical profession gotten so cold?

As she limped to her recliner, her phone beeped. For a second, she thought it might be the doctor's office calling back, then realized it was a text. Her first incoming communication since the strike. She opened the icon and read the message from Chris: *Want to hang out? Pizza and bowling at Mac's?*

Pizza sounded great, but bowling with a burned butt… She smiled at her own predicament, a little surprised that she knew how to bowl. Her body wasn't exactly athletic. She also didn't know who Chris was. A boyfriend? In the moment, it didn't matter. She wasn't going out.

She texted back: *Hey, sorry but I can't. I got hit by lightning a few days ago and it hurts to walk.* Remi laughed. That had to be the lamest, or weirdest, excuse ever.

Chris: *U joking?*

She'd expected that. But what now? Invite them over? *No.* She wasn't ready. Remi keyed in: *For real. But I need a few more days to recover.*

Chris: *Feel better. I'll bring pizza when you're ready. Tell me about the lightning thing. I want details.*

Remi smiled. Chris was either a woman or a gay man. She texted that she was too tired and would describe it all later. She had mixed feelings about seeing anyone, but she didn't feel particularly lonely. Maybe she was one of those people who lived alone and liked it fine.

She stroked Tuck's head. "Except for you, buddy."

Remi opened her text app again and discovered the only messages were the ones she'd just exchanged. Either she had never texted before—unlikely as hell —or she'd deleted all her messages after reading them. That was either nutcase paranoid or a compulsive ADD behavior. Considering the cash in the safe and lack of a bank account, paranoia seemed to be her operating mode. A sad thought. Now she worried that her fears would return with her memories And she probably lived alone because she was too quirky for most people. But the little boy at the daycare had seemed quite fond of her, so at least she'd done her job well.

Remi turned on the TV. A morning news anchor was yakking about some rich guy buying Twitter. After a few soundbites, the reporter referenced Facebook and Instagram too. Social media platforms that sounded familiar. Remi had no specific memory of using them, but she understood how they worked, so she assumed she had accounts. Maybe looking at what she'd posted would help trigger a few memories. She checked her phone, but didn't find any icons. She wasn't on social media either? How much of a paranoid recluse was she? A vague sense of dread washed over her. This wasn't just about being a conspiracy nut or antisocial. She was afraid of someone finding her. That was why she didn't have an online presence or financial accounts or a rental contract.

Oh hell. She'd been so out of it, she'd forgotten to take the rent money to Izzy. Walking up the driveway sounded like pure torture, but she would force herself. She texted Izzy: *You home? Bringing the rent.*

Her landlord quickly replied: *about time.* Followed by a smiley face.

Remi shuffled to the kitchen, pulled the envelope from the junk drawer where she'd stashed it, and headed for the door. Tuck ran ahead, wagging his tail.

"Yes, we're leaving the house. I know how exciting this is for you." She felt bad she hadn't walked him since the lightning strike. She hadn't danced either and she missed it. Even listening to music was frustrating because her body wanted to move, but it was just too excruciating.

Halfway up the long driveway, she had to stop and take a break. She'd been making a strange half-grunt, half-moan sound, and Tuck was distressed for her. "I'm okay, boy. But I gotta keep moving. This is how I'll heal."

Remi forced herself to walk again.

When she approached the house, Izzy stood in the open door. "I would have come down for it."

"I appreciate that, but I've been sleeping and resting too much. That's why I spaced off the rent. Sorry about that."

"No problem." The old lady narrowed her eyes. "You're sweatin' and lookin' kinda peaked. You okay?"

"Not really. I'm in hella pain."

Izzy made a tsking sound. "Didn't they give somethin' for that?"

"Not enough. I ran out last night and can't get more until I see my doctor next week."

"That sucks." A long pause. "Maybe I can help you." A door

banged shut in the background. "My cousin, a veteran, has a methadone prescription. But he doesn't take as many as they give him, so he sells half to make ends meet."

It sounded shady, but Remi didn't care. "It works for pain? I thought it was for addicts to get clean."

"It's also a potent pain killer and easier on the stomach than others."

"Great. I'll take whatever he's willing to let go of."

"If you've got another hundred in cash, I'll get 'em when I go out for groceries."

Thank god. Remi almost cried with relief.

Chapter 8

The Recent Past
My head felt like it would explode

Aug. 1 (day 29 after the strike)

Remi walked up the driveway with Tuck at her side, loving the feel of the sun on her face before it got too warm. Her pain was easing a little, and she was determined to take poor doggo out every day. They'd been to the park once, but the effort had exhausted her, so she was sticking closer to home. Almost a month since the lightning strike, and she was still struggling… to walk normally, to dance, to wake up without a headache, to remember her life before this town. Yet, after one follow-up visit, Dr. Sanjay had declared her "physically fine except for the burns, which were healing nicely."

What the hell did he know?

She reached her landlord's house and called through the screen door, "Izzy? I have the rent."

"Be right there," the woman called from deep in the house. "Or just come on in."

Remi stepped inside. Since the strike, she'd eaten dinner with Izzy and her cousin a few times and felt at home. The food wasn't her favorite, but she liked the company. A pang of guilt made her wince. She'd brushed off her friend Chris several times because she couldn't bring herself to admit to him or her that they were a stranger.

Izzy trudged into the living room and reached down to pet Tuck. "Gonna be a hot one today."

"Better than cold." Remi smiled. They'd had this conversation a few times. She held out the cash envelope. "The extra hundred is in there." Her third methadone purchase.

Izzy handed her a small plastic bottle. "You gotta be careful with this stuff girl. It's addictive."

"How?" Remi scowled. "It doesn't even get me high. It just keeps the pain and anxiety under control." The medicine suppressed her headaches too and, she had to admit, muted her emotions with a gauze-like effect.

The older woman shook her gray afro. "Don't be a ditz. Methadone is an opioid; of course it's addictive. Time to start cuttin' back. Maybe break the pills in half."

"Yes, mom." Remi chuckled.

So did Izzy. "It's good to see you smile." A pause. "But hey, I'm serious. It's powerful stuff and it might be messin' with you getting all your memory back."

"Hmm." Remi didn't believe it. She'd recalled some of her life in Wilsonville, it was just further back that was blank. It was odd how she remembered all the functionality stuff about life, but not the personal details, as though they were stored in a different place in her brain. "Hey, can I do anything for you while I'm here?" She'd been helping Izzy with chores that required strong hands. Anything to feel useful.

"Yeah, I have to clean the skylight and need help getting the glass down."

"Sure." Remi followed her into the quaint kitchen that always smelled wonderful. A pot was on the stove. "What's in the soup?"

"A little bit of everything. Leftovers mostly." Izzy ladled two scoops into a plastic container. "To take with you." She tapped the lid. "I want this back."

"Of course. Thank you."

When they finished the project, Remi headed back to her house. She'd intended to walk farther, but she wanted to take a pill first. After missing her morning dose, her pain and frustration were building to the point of irritability. She always kept it lighthearted with Izzy, but most of the time she felt trapped in a life she didn't recognize or like very much.

Memories of her house and job were slowly coming back, yet none of it felt right. Whatever her life had been before she lived in this town seemed to be erased from her mind. Yet her past still had a tight grip on how she lived now. She wanted to put the cash from the safe into a bank account and use a credit card to pay for groceries like everyone else did. But she didn't have either convenience and she was afraid to open any accounts. She'd obviously avoided the financial world before lightning ruined her, and Remi trusted her previous self to know what she was doing. Vague fear still hovered over her. Someone, somewhere, she couldn't remember specifically, scared her.

Tuck ran ahead and waited by their front door. "Hey! I count on you to protect me." Remi chuckled. He was too small and friendly to be any use as a guard dog.

In the house, she stood in the kitchen and stared at the bottle of pills she'd just bought. If not for Tuck, she might be tempted—late some night when everything seemed bleakest—to take the whole handful and just end it. Once again, he was saving her life.

What the hell did that mean? She had no idea.

Remi opened the bottle, swallowed a tablet with some diet Dr. Pepper, then moved to her recliner and got out her phone. In addition to the dreariness of her current life, at times she felt grief-stricken with a sense of loss, possibly for her other life. Remi wanted to get past all of it. Time to call the counselor in her contacts and make an appointment.

After only two rings, a woman picked up. "This is Joanne."

Startled that she'd actually answered, Remi stuttered. "Uh, this is Remi Bartel. I found your name in my phone contacts."

"Remi. Good to hear from you. How are you?"

"Not optimal."

"I'm sorry to hear that." Sounds of a chair scooting. "I had a no-show, so I have some time right now. What's going on? Is your guilt troubling you again?"

What guilt? "I was hit by lightning."

The counselor gasped. "Wow. I have no idea what that does to your body or mental health, but I'm glad you called."

"I lost most of my memory." Remi unexpectedly burst into tears. When she got herself under control, she summed up what she'd been through and was still experiencing—but didn't mention the methadone. That situation was temporary and nobody needed to know.

"Memory isn't my field of expertise, but I have a few ideas we can try." Joanne sounded upbeat.

"I'm game. I can't live like this."

"I have an opening next Wednesday at ten. Can you make that?"

"Sure. See you then."

At first, Remi felt relieved to know she would be talking to a counselor. But the more she thought about it, the more anxiety set in. She'd obviously told Joanne about her past, and there was something from that time to feel guilty about. Did she really want to know? She had enough stress just dealing with chronic pain and fatigue. Why dredge up old trauma? Maybe she would cancel the appointment.

Remi turned on the TV, hoping the methadone would kick in soon, then paused the talk show almost immediately. The guilt might only be a small part of whatever her life had been. She wanted to know the rest, especially about any family she might have. Maybe she would keep the session and try the counselor's suggestions.

Her phone beeped and she checked the ID. *Cheri*, from the daycare. Remi forced herself to take the call. She'd ignored several of her employer's voicemails already. "Hey, Cheri."

"Hi, Remi. How are you?"

"Better, but still in pain."

A long pause.

"When do you think you might be back?"

"I don't know." The reason she'd been avoiding the conversation.

"I'm sorry, but I think we have to hire a permanent replacement for you." Cheri let out a breath she'd been holding. "But we'll take you back if an opening comes up in the future."

"I understand. I'm sorry about the inconvenience."

"It's okay. Just take care of yourself. And come visit us when you feel better. The kids miss you."

"Tell them I said hello. Bye."

Now she was officially unemployed—and burning through the cash in the safe. Maybe she should file for disability. *Yeah, right.* Her doctor thought she was "fine." Other people had been through worse, she reminded herself. In fact, other people had probably been through the same experience. Maybe they had figured out strategies for healing themselves. Remi opened the browser on her phone and googled *lightning strike survivors*.

The third link after two news stories took her to a page labeled *LS & ESSI, Lightning Strike and Electrical Shock Survivors International.* She skimmed the brief *About* page. They had two thousand members and held a yearly conference in March, which they recorded and shared on the website. At the bottom of the page, she followed a link to Wikipedia that claimed 240,000 lightning incidents occurred around the world each year, a statistic that didn't include the people who'd been shocked by powerlines or other high-voltage equipment.

Good grief! A lot of people had been through this shit. Remi clicked back to the support group, then opened another tab. The page had information about preventing lightning strikes, but nothing about healing from one. She scrolled down and read a few personal stories. One woman's quote stood out: *The left side of my head felt like it would explode.*

Her own morning headache didn't seem so bad now. Or maybe that was just the methadone finally kicking in.

Another tab listed a dozen locations where small support groups met regularly. One was in southwest Portland, only a twenty-five-minute drive. She scanned the site for a date. Their next meeting was two days away. Remi felt a surge of dread. *Too soon.* She wasn't ready to drive that far. Yet she really wanted to talk about this fucked-up experience with other people who could relate.

She decided to go. What did she have to lose, except a few hours?

Chapter 9

The Turbulent Present
You got the DTs

Sept. 8, Portland (day 1 after the kidnapping)

Remi woke with her usual headache and a fog of confusion. *Where the hell was she?* Oh yeah, a storage room in a B&B rental, somewhere north. She'd been awake and terrified half the night that the men would barge in and rape her. When she'd finally drifted off, one nightmare after another had plagued her.

She sat up and promptly vomited on the floor. *Gah!* What the hell was that about? She desperately needed to rinse her mouth, but the narrow room was empty except for a foam pad and thin blanket. She'd asked for a bottle of water as Blake locked her in the night before, but he'd laughed and said, "There's no toilet in there, so maybe not."

Now she really had to pee. Remi struggled to her feet, the only light coming from under the door. Once she was upright, she started to shake. And her intestines were on fire. What was happening? She stepped to the door and pounded. "Hey, I need help!"

No response.

She tried again, then leaned against the wall. Had she caught a crazy new virus?

Footsteps in the hall, then Seth called out, "Get away from the door."

"I need to pee."

"Just step back while I open it. I don't want trouble."

"Okay." She felt too sick to do anything but whine.

Seth came into the room and held out a zip-tie.

"Can it wait until after I use the bathroom?" She hated asking and hated being at his mercy even more. "You have my dog, remember? And I'm sick."

They both glanced at the vomit.

"After I puked, I started shaking." Another stab of belly pain hit her. Remi moaned and doubled over.

"Your guts hurt too?" Seth gave her a weird look.

"Maybe it's food poisoning." They'd fed her a PBJ and stale potato chips for dinner, so not likely.

"You been on pain meds? Like oxy or a fen patch?"

"Yeah, why?"

"You haven't dosed since we picked you up. You got the DTs."

What? For a moment, she didn't know what he meant. Then she realized she was in withdrawal from methadone. Oh, great, frosting on the shit-cake of her life. Izzy had warned her about addiction, but not about the hell of quitting abruptly. Neither of them had counted on her being kidnapped.

First things first. "I need to pee. Now."

Leaving her hands free, Seth led her to a closet-sized bathroom, then leaned close to whisper. "I've got some Vicodin that will head this off for now. We need you in good shape tonight."

He lowered his voice another notch. "Let's keep this on the down low, K? Blake doesn't need to know."

Remi nodded. To stay alive, she needed to be useful to them.

"Be right back." Seth stepped out and closed the door.

It wasn't until a few moments later when she got up from the toilet that she realized she was unbound and unguarded. Was this her chance to make a break for the front door? Maybe she could get the police here before they had a chance to hurt Tuck. More likely, Blake was sitting in the living room with his gun. She visualized him shooting her. If or when he did, would they cut her up in the bathtub and stuff her into a suitcase? Or roll her up in an area rug and haul her out like garbage?

She thought about the cash in her safe at home. Should she try to buy her way out? *No.* Not unless they specifically mentioned it. If that money was what these thugs wanted, they would've taken it instead of her. Or they might have already taken it before they picked her up.

As Remi stepped toward the sink, her stomach roiled and she vomited again. With a shaky hand, she splashed water into her mouth, then stared at herself in the mirror. *Gah!* Paler than usual, pinpoint pupils, and a glimmer of sweat under her eyes. She hadn't known withdrawal could be like this. If she survived this ordeal, she would never take methadone again. Or maybe any opioids. But how would she live with the damage to her body? Some people used cannabis for chronic pain, but she didn't want to get high every day just to survive.

A loud rap on the door. "I'm comin' in."

Remi turned and Seth was in the room.

"What were ya takin'?"

It took a moment to realize what he was asking. "Methadone."

He raised an eyebrow. "No wonder. How much and how often?"

"Half a pill first thing in the morning, then the rest in the late afternoon. I think the whole thing is forty milligrams." She was glad she'd started breaking them in half, like Izzy had suggested.

"That's a lot of dolly." Seth held out two white tablets. "Take these. I'll give ya more this afternoon."

She swallowed the pills with tap water from her palm. Anything to feel better. "I think I need something in my stomach."

Seth abruptly swung a fist at her gut.

Remi sucked in and braced for it.

At the last inch, he pulled back. "Just fuckin' with ya. As a reminder."

She pressed her lips to keep her smart mouth in check. Maybe Seth and Blake would go out for burgers and get obliterated by a semi-truck.

He held out a zip-tie. "Break's over. Time to start preppin' for tonight."

Chapter 10

The Turbulent Present
He patted her down thoroughly

Late that afternoon

As the van slowed, Remi's pulse accelerated. What she was about to do made her nervous as hell. She felt unqualified on every level. But since she had no choice, she tried to play it down. *No big deal,* she kept telling herself. She would just serve food and drinks and listen to a conversation. Nothing difficult, illegal, or dangerous. Except for the men who held Tuck captive and threatened to kill him and her mother if she ran away or screwed up. The screwup is what scared her—being caught eavesdropping or performing so badly on the job they would know she wasn't a real server. The worst the dinner guys could do was throw her out or call the police, but her kidnappers...

From the floor in the back, Remi peered out the front window of the van. They were in a parking lot behind a seven-story hotel. On the drive here, she'd caught enough of the cityscape to believe they'd driven from a suburb into downtown Portland.

"Ready?" Blake asked.

"I hope so." She was dressed in black pants that were too tight and a white button-up shirt that was too hot. "I've never tested my memory skills, so I can't guarantee anything." Another reminder to downplay their expectations.

The big guy pinched her cheek. "Your life depends on it." He handed her a name-tag. "To clock in, scan the barcode on the back."

The ID said *Riley*. Blake had called her that once too, and she'd thought it was a mistake. "Why Riley?"

"That's your real name." He stared at her through narrowed eyes. "Faking amnesia won't buy you any leeway with Yano."

Remi clenched her teeth. "I was hit by lightning! And I've been in a fog ever since. I don't know jackshit about Yano or who I used to be."

"I'm sure he'll find ways to remind you."

Another man who would hurt her. "Yano? What kind of name is that anyway?"

"Short for Sebastiano. Does that help?"

"No."

"Let's do this." Blake slid a sharp blade between her bound wrists. "Last warning before I cut the zip-tie. If you stray from your instructions, even in the smallest way, your dog dies a slow painful death."

Remi believed him. "I'll do exactly what you want," she said through clenched teeth. She hated being compliant. She glanced over at the hotel. Maybe she would just go to the roof and jump, avoid the slow heinous death Yano had in mind.

"You need to report back every single word they say. Every company mentioned, every stock, every buy order."

"Got it." They'd been over this repeatedly. "Then you'll let me go?"

"Not my call." He cut the plastic tie. "If Yano makes a chunk of his money back, he might spare your life." Blake leaned in close. "If he loses his investment, *your* death will be torture too."

"I can only tell you what they say."

Blake rose, still hunched over in the cargo van, and yanked her to her feet. "Do not fuck this up. Things could get worse." He opened the sliding door. "We have all the hotel exits covered, so don't even think about running." He stepped out and Remi followed.

As they walked past employee vehicles toward the back loading area, Remi glanced around. This was her chance to run. But she wouldn't get far. Her butt cheek still ached and she felt weak and shaky. Seth's pills weren't as strong as the methadone and her body wasn't happy about it. Besides, her sweet little Tuck was still drugged and caged in the B&B. She wouldn't abandon him. The thought made her wonder if anyone had reported her missing. Maybe Chris.

As they neared the door, a young male employee jogged past. "Better hurry. The prep meeting starts in five."

Blake gave her a shove. "Do not disappoint us."

Remi scurried to the banged-up metal door. Beside it, a wide overhead door started to open, and she heard a truck backing up. The sounds and sequences all felt vaguely familiar. Inside the back of the hotel, she looked left for the time clock. As directed, she held the name-tag to the electric eye and the device pinged, clocking her in. She pinned the tag above her left breast. Step one, complete.

She hurried up the hall past a cluster of small offices and caught up to the guy who'd spoken to her earlier and had now stopped to check his phone. His tag said *Marco*. "Can I follow you? I'm new."

"We're here." He turned into an employee breakroom crowded with people, all dressed in black and white. Most were in their twenties and thirties, and the women were slender and pretty. Remi felt like an obvious imposter. A guy in a suit jacket stood at the front and read a list of names, but not hers. "You're all working the banquet in the big ballroom on the fourth floor. You know the drill. Once you have the tables set, check with the kitchen to see what prep work is left."

Most of the crowd filed out, leaving Remi and Marco. The manager nodded at them. "You two are working the VIP meeting in the private dining room." He narrowed his eyes at Remi. "I haven't seen you before."

"I'm with Culinary Temps, filling in for Jenny tonight." It was true, but felt like a lie.

"Oh hell. This gig needs someone with experience."

Remi swallowed hard. "I've been in food and cocktail service for twelve years." According to Blake, that had been true at one point.

The manager nodded. "You know the rules for these VIPs?"

"No phones or other electronics." She assumed her captors had taken hers, along with her purse. Remi stepped toward the manager.

He patted her down thoroughly, squatting to make sure she didn't have a phone tucked into her socks. When he stood, he stared at her face. "Have you got any makeup with you?"

"No. Sorry." Remi blushed with shame, hating every man on the planet.

"The women's bathroom has a basket with a bunch of odds and ends. There should be some mascara or blush you can put on." The manager waved her away. "Get moving."

Forty minutes later, she carried a tray of cocktails across a private dining room on the top floor. In one corner was a small bar service, where Marco had made the drinks, and the long exterior wall featured floor-to-ceiling windows overlooking the city lights. The men, wearing button-down shirts, sat on a plush, L-shaped sofa near a round dining table.

"Bourbon, neat." Remi set down a tumbler next to a guy in his late fifties. Blake had coached her with their names and online images, so she recognized the handsome man as Senator James Mercer. He was the one with the most vital information.

Mercer was talking and didn't even look up. "So on the ninth hole, I go to putt and…"

She processed all of it, even though the subject was golf, not stocks or trades. Blake had stressed "every word." Remi set a tall glass in front of the oldest guy, Matt Cartwright, a hedge fund manager, whatever that was. "Rum and diet coke, lots of ice."

The third man, a fifty-something banker named Rashib Patel, who bulged out of his shirt, had ordered a dry martini. She set it in front of him and started to walk back to her position. Patel grabbed her left butt cheek, and she almost screamed.

Jackass!

"Where are my extra olives? And where's Jenny?" He glared, seriously annoyed.

"She's out sick. I'm Rem—, Riley, and I'll go get more." She turned to leave again.

"Take the drink and get it right."

With the senator still talking about golf, Remi picked up the cocktail and walked away, glad this was a one-time gig. How had she done this for a living for over a decade? The rhythm of it was familiar and easy, but the subservience was hard to take. Worried that she would miss vital conversation, she tried to hurry, but the pain made it awkward. Blake had said they wouldn't "get to the serious shit until they cut into their steaks."

Marco wasn't behind the service bar, so she stabbed three green olives on a toothpick and added it to the martini glass. She started to turn back, then spotted a small knife on a cutting board with some limes. Impulsively, she grabbed the knife and shoved it into her pants pocket. On the way back, she tried to visualize how she would keep the knife hidden or what Blake would do if he discovered it, then she almost tossed it aside as not worth the trouble. But she couldn't bring herself to let go of it. Not yet.

At the table, she served the drink again, then moved to her position against a nearby wall, close enough that they didn't have to raise their voices to summon her and she could hear almost everything they said. The men yakked about golf for another ten minutes and she felt herself drifting. She'd never been tasked with anything like this and doubted her ability to recall every word. After another five minutes of chatter about their busy schedules, the guys got up and moved to the table. That was her cue, and she headed for the service bar again.

Their meals had been preordered, and she brought a shrimp cocktail platter from the mini fridge with their second round of drinks. The only time she would leave the room was to fetch their hot dinner plates from the nearby kitchen. Their conversation shifted to sexual encounters and Remi felt her face flush. The fat guy who'd grabbed her was a crude misogynist.

After her trip to the kitchen to serve the main course, Remi stepped back, her stomach growling from the smell of grilled meat. This time, she stayed a little closer. The next twenty minutes were crucial and she was worried. She'd been on her feet for an hour and her whole body hurt. The second dose of Vicodin Seth had given her was wearing off, and she could feel the shakes coming on.

The hedge fund guy shifted into a serious tone. "What's the update on the energy bill? Did you get the oil leases added?"

This was it! Remi tuned out everything—her body-ache, the lights shimmering on the glass wall, the hum of conversation in the ballroom next door—and focused on every word.

Chapter 11

The Turbulent Present

Hot wives in important positions

Minutes later

To get closer, she filled their water glasses as the senator responded. "No, but McClaren squeezed in a half-billion-dollar investment in a couple of clean-energy startups, so they're a buy and hold." Mercer paused to chew and swallow. "Windstar and EnvoFuel."

The other men picked up their phones and keyed in the information.

"That's worth a six-figure donation." Patel gave a sleazy smile.

"Any short-term tips?" the hedge fund guy asked.

Mercer grinned. "My wife says the FDA just approved a gene therapy for diabetes, a potential blockbuster. Made by a little biotech called Genovics. It's trading at sixteen dollars a share, but when the announcement hits the news in the next day or so, the value will skyrocket."

"Sweet!" Cartwright raised his cocktail. "To hot wives in important positions."

The men laughed, sipped their drinks, and resumed eating.

A moment later, the banker grumbled, "My side dishes are

cold." He held up his hand and snapped his fingers. "Take my plate to the kitchen and have it heated."

Damn! Remi hurried forward, grimacing. She didn't want to leave and miss any financial tips. Hand shaking, she picked up Patel's plate. *Please don't let it bang against his drink.* As she stepped back and pivoted to leave, her left glute seized up. Remi stumbled and the plate flew out of her hand. *Fuck!* She landed on one knee, then struggled to push back up.

"What the hell is wrong with you?" Patel snapped. "You took forever bringing our food and now you can't walk without tripping."

"I'm so sorry," Remi gushed. "My leg cramped. I'll get you a new meal."

"No. You're done. Just get out and send in someone competent." The banker pointed at the side exit.

"That's a little harsh," the senator said, then laughed.

Marco, the bartender, rushed over and gathered the scattered asparagus that had rolled. "We'll comp your dinner, sir."

"You'd better. And get this clumsy chub out of here."

Blinking back tears, Remi shuffled away. *Such a prick!*

As she shuffled into the staff hall, panicked thoughts bounced around her head. Blake would kill her for getting booted before the conversation was over. She should just head for the basement, then run. Or realistically, limp-walk as best she could to find help. *No.* They had the exits covered. And they still had Tuck. Maybe she wouldn't tell them she'd been eighty-sixed. She could say the dinner had ended early.

Functioning on autopilot, Remi took the service elevator down to the main floor and exited the building the way she'd come in. Fully dark now, she felt disoriented for a moment. Then a reverse image of the layout came to her. She headed in the opposite direction of the loading bay.

Blake stepped out from behind a dumpster and grabbed her arm. "You're early. What happened?" He half led, half dragged her across the parking lot.

"Uh." She wanted to lie, but she was in so much pain, she couldn't pull it off. "My glute cramped and I stumbled. Patel, who'd been rude to me all evening, yelled for me to get out."

"Oh fuck." The big guy struck the back of her head with an open palm. "Did you get any financial chatter at all?"

"Yes." Her spine seemed to reverberate from the blow and Remi clenched her fists. She remembered the knife in her pocket and thought seriously about stabbing Blake. But the paring blade was only about four inches long and she would have to plunge it into his neck to even faze the big man.

"Stop draggin'." He yanked on her arm.

Remi tried to pick up her pace.

When they reached the van, Blake shoved her into the back, climbed in behind her, and zip-tied her wrists. Kneeling by her side, he pulled his phone and made a call. "Let's go."

Seth showed up a few minutes later, and Remi wondered which door he'd been watching. Did they have anyone else or had that been bullshit? The hotel had at least four entrances. Not that it mattered. They had Tuck and she wouldn't abandon him.

As they entered the road, Blake backhanded her in the face. "I told you not to fuck it up."

Remi bit the inside of her cheeks so hard she tasted blood. "I'm sure I got what you need, and the timing of the trade is critical. So let me tell you before you knock my teeth out."

"I'm listening." Blake sat back, cross-legged. "Just the important part right now. Save the rest for later."

The specific line of conversation played in her mind. "The senator said the FDA had approved a gene therapy developed by Genovics and to buy it now before the announcement. He expects the value to skyrocket." She used quote gestures around the last word.

"You're sure?"

Remi nodded.

Blake squeezed her thigh. He might have meant it like a pat on the head, but the gesture was painful, like every time he touched her. Especially her face, which felt deeply bruised. Remi vowed to free herself and Tuck, then hurt Blake on her way out.

He made another call. "Hey, Yano. I've got a hot tip straight from Senator Mercer." Blake chuckled. "At least according to your old friend, Riley."

A pause.

"Buy Genovics ASAP. I'll call you with more later." Blake hung up.

"The stock market is closed right now, isn't it?" Remi didn't know much about finance, but she'd heard the term *closing bell* at some point in her life.

"We can put in buy orders that will go through first thing tomorrow, East Coast time."

The big guy seemed happy for the moment, and Remi wanted to feel hopeful that this might soon be over. But she doubted they would just let her go. She could identify them. Maybe that didn't matter. She just had to convince Blake that the threat of him knowing where she lived was enough to guarantee her silence. "Once you hear my whole report, you can release me. I swear I'll never tell anyone. I'd be too scared." She wouldn't even say the word *police*.

Blake laughed. "You wish. Yano wants the two of you to get reacquainted."

Chapter 12

The Recent Past
The shock blew off my arms

Aug. 3, Wilsonville (day 31 after the strike)

Remi pulled on a teal-colored blouse and turned to look at herself in the full-length mirror. The shirt hung to the top of her legs, covering the area where her body bulged out of her black yoga pants. *Not bad.* Still, jeans might make a better first impression. *No.* They were too uncomfortable to drive in, especially now that she'd gained a few pounds. She tried to forgive herself. Exercising with a burned butt was asking too much. The methadone helped, but it wasn't a miracle cure.

In the bathroom, she applied foundation and mascara, the only makeup in the drawer. As she dabbed at her short lashes, a sense of *deja vu*—or was it memory?— paralyzed her for a moment. Sometime in her past, she'd stared into a magnified mirror to put on makeup, obsessing over the eyeliner. Not a helpful memory, but at least they were still breaking through on occasion.

In the kitchen, she picked up her purse and looked down at Tuck. "Want to go for a ride?"

He wiggled excitedly and ran for the front door. She hoped

it was okay to take him into the meeting. If not, he could wait in the car.

On the drive to the freeway, Remi passed a big metal building with a sign that said *Bartel's Meat Packing*. Odd that she shared the name. Was the business owned by a relative? Is that why she'd settled here? A stranger thought hit her. What if she had driven by years ago and chosen the surname? Then what? She had a driver's license that said *Remi Lynn Bartel*. Was it fake? To legally change her name, she would've had to visit a social security office and show her original birth certificate—which was probably in the safe deposit box she couldn't locate. If she had officially changed her name, that was some serious shit, an all-out effort to make her old self disappear. The counselor's mention of guilt haunted her. What if she had done something awful and it had gone viral? That could've been enough to need a fresh start. Yet it didn't explain her use of cash only. And it didn't account for her fear and grief either. Her one counseling session, focused on recovering her memories, had been a bust. She might try again, but for now, she hoped the support group would have suggestions for how to cope.

The trip took longer than she'd budgeted, and as she pulled into the parking lot, she had second thoughts about the meeting. She hated walking in late. Everyone would turn and look at her. And the building, an old grange with peeling white paint, gave off a bad vibe. But damn, she'd endured Portland traffic to get here. Remi grabbed her purse and looked at Tuck. "Let's do this."

She willed herself to get out of the Mazda, promising herself a treat on the way home. Maybe a scoop of ice cream to cool her off. The heat was working its way toward ninety. She stepped inside and took in a deep breath. *Ugh.* The foyer smelled funky, as if it had once been flooded. Almost a dealbreaker. But she kept moving. A rolling chalkboard listed the meeting in room #2, with an arrow pointing left. Very helpful. Did that mean the groupies were all forgetful? They probably didn't get new members very often.

The door was partly open, and someone inside was speaking. Remi sucked in her gut and stepped in. Six people sat in folding chairs arranged in a circle. As expected, they all turned to her—but they were smiling.

"I'm sorry I'm late."

"It's all good." A forty-something woman stood and pointed to an empty chair. "Welcome. I'm Alicia."

"Remi." She glanced down. "This is Tuck. Can he stay? If not, he's okay in the car."

Alicia looked around the circle, and the groupies all shrugged or nodded. One woman called doggo "cute."

After she sat, she made a point to look at each member and smile. Remi regretted her decision to be here. The only person her age was a man with no arms. One of his shoulder stumps had a metal prosthetic, but his sleeve on the other side just hung there. *Oh god.* It made her heart hurt just to look at him.

"I'm Gary," he said with a grin. "And yes, this was caused by electricity. When I was ten, I climbed a utility pole. I either did something stupid, or it malfunctioned, and the shock blew off my arms."

Remi swallowed and tried to think of the right thing to say. Empathy first, then move on. "I'm sorry that happened. But it's nice to meet you."

"It's good to have you here." Gary turned to the old guy with a gray ponytail next to him. "This is Doug. He got shocked on the job."

Doug nodded and Remi nodded back. "Hi."

The other three members, all fifty or older, introduced themselves and she easily remembered their names. Her new ability to recall everything she read or heard still surprised her. In this moment, it was useful, but otherwise not so much. She would have gladly traded it to know her own past.

"Since you're new, tell us your story," Alicia said. "We've heard all of ours a few times."

The spotlight was on her already. "There's not much to tell. I was outside with my daycare kids and got hit by lightning."

"Was it your first strike?" asked Marta, a pretty woman to her right.

Startled, Remi turned to face her. "What? You mean people get zapped more than once?"

"I've been hit twice, ten years apart." Marta tapped a piece of beige plastic behind her ear. "That's why I wear these. I also lost my sense of smell after the second one."

They were all suffering! Their collective anguish washed over her and Remi fought back tears. What she intended to do was express sympathy, but instead she blurted, "I lost my memory."

"Oh no."

"All of it?"

"You poor thing."

Tears rolled down her cheeks and her body shook with silent sobs. Not even her counselor had understood or empathized in this way. Tuck jumped to his feet and whimpered loudly. Remi fought for control. "I'm sorry."

"Never apologize for grief," Marta said softly.

Grief? Yes, she was grieving the loss of herself and whoever she had been. "Thank you. I appreciate your kindness. All of you."

"That's why we're here." Gary stood. "Want a hug?"

With that metal thing? Remi struggled to find the right response. Alicia gestured for him to sit back down. "Too soon."

"I can ballroom dance as well." Gary grinned. "At the end of the meeting, I'll demonstrate, if you're willing."

Remi smiled. She liked this guy's energy and confidence.

"What's it been like for you?" Marta asked. "I mean, with symptoms and doctors and family and all that." Her tone held a sense of expectation.

"The ER doc who treated me says I'm fine." Their last conversation played in Remi's mind. "But I have headaches, and my burns are still quite painful. Yet he won't give me any more pain meds."

The members all nodded and murmured in a knowing way.

"When were you struck? And what about your memory loss?" Alicia prodded.

"A month ago." Remi shifted in her chair, still surprised to be the group's focus. "Some of my recent memory has come back. Little things that happened in my house, plus I remember a few kids from the daycare." She paused, a familiar stress building. "But I can't recall anything personal before I moved to my current home a few years ago."

"What about friends and coworkers?" Marta looked concerned.

Remi shook her head.

"How is your family taking it? Are they supportive?"

Remi pressed her lips together, holding back another wave of

60

tears. "I don't seem to have any family. Or at least none of them have called to check on me."

Marta leaned over and gave Remi a shoulder hug. "We'll be your family."

Remi patted her hand. "Thanks." She looked at Alicia, who seemed to be the group leader. "I don't mean to take up the whole meeting. What else do you guys usually do?"

Alicia shrugged. "We talk about our lives, especially anything that relates to the afterstrike effects."

Gary rocked forward. "We play cards sometimes too."

A memory surfaced, and Remi smiled. "I just recalled playing Uno with the kids. Such a fun way for them to learn numbers and colors."

"We play gin rummy." Gary waved his metal claw. "I'm hard on the cards, but I'm unbeatable."

"We'll see." Remi was feeling better than she had since that day. "Another weird thing that happened with my brain is how the strike affected my current memory. I recall everything I read or see."

"Like hyperthymesia?" Alicia's eyes narrowed with skepticism.

"Sort of, except mine only pertains to anything after the lightning." Remi had done a bit of online research, but her headaches limited her screen time.

"That's weird, but cool." Gary beamed at her again.

Was he flirting?

Footsteps in the hall made them all turn toward the door. A tall woman with wavy auburn hair and a large shoulder bag stood in the doorway.

Alicia got up. "I meant to remind everyone that the reporter would be here today." She turned to Remi. "I hope that's okay. We set it up at our last meeting."

Chapter 13

The Recent Past

Such a charmer, and so hard to say no to

Moments later

Remi shifted nervously, instinct telling her to leave, but she couldn't make herself. These people were special and she wanted to be part of the group. "I don't want my name or photo used, but I'd like to stay and hear the conversations." If she didn't use her name on bank accounts or rental contracts, she sure as hell didn't want it in the paper.

"That's fine." Alicia waved the reporter in. "This is Serena Townsend, from the Portland Tribune."

As they were introduced, the members got to their feet, some rather slowly, and shook the reporter's hand. When Alicia got to Remi, she said, "As you probably heard, our new member isn't ready to participate."

"No problem." Serena smiled, then pivoted back to the group. "I'd like to just sit and listen while you all tell your stories, then afterward, I'll ask some individual questions." She paused to pull a camera from her shoulder bag. "I'll take photos as I go along, then get everyone together for a group shot before I leave. Sound okay?"

Alicia looked around and the group seemed excited, except Doug, who only shrugged.

Gary waved his metal claw. "I'd like to go first."

Remi had just heard his story, so she reached down and petted Tuck, stroking behind his ears. "Good boy," she whispered. He jumped into her lap, and she smiled. This wasn't her recliner, and he was too big to get comfortable, but she let him stay for a minute.

Gary started talking about his childhood struggles and what it was like before schools made an effort to accommodate students with disabilities.

The reporter soon cut him off. "I'll get back to you with some one-on-one questions."

Gary winked at the young woman. "I'll hold you to it."

After listening to the group talk about the electrical shocks that changed their lives, Remi was ready for a break. Their collective trauma was overwhelming. Doug had lost his job, his wife and kids, and his life savings. Marta had been more fortunate with her husband and family, but she now suffered seizures and couldn't drive or hold a job. And poor Zeph had been struck in the head and lost an eye. He also had nerve damage and struggled to retain information.

"The opposite of Remi's situation," Zeph said, smiling at her. "She lost her memory of the past, but she recalls everything she learns now."

The reporter turned to her, and Remi sucked in her breath. "Please don't mention me."

"I won't use your name, but I would like to hear more." Sere-

na brought her chair over and sat by Remi. "Just a few questions."
She smiled warmly.

Such a charmer, and so hard to say no to. "All right."

"Were you hit in the head like Zeph and Marta?" The reporter pressed a record button on her phone.

"I don't think so. I have a burn in my shoulder-socket"—Remi
touched the still-tender area—"where I assume the lightning entered, and a burn on my butt cheek where it exited."

"That must be painful."

Remi nodded. "I feel like I'll never walk normally again."

"Tell me about your memory issues."

"At first, I was a blank and didn't even know my own name.
That was terrifying." Her first moments in the hospital played in
her mind, and Remi tensed. "But some recent memories have
started to come back, so I'm encouraged." She gave a tight smile.

"Is that why you don't want your name published?"

"Sort of."

"What about the new recall? Is that like photographic memory?"

"Not really. For me, it's about words that I hear or read. If I'm
concentrating, I can remember them all."

The reporter looked surprised. "For how long?"

"I don't know. I've never tested it." Remi shifted to ease the
pressure on her left glute.

"Can I call you again in a month or so for a follow-up?"

Remi hesitated. "I suppose."

"Thanks for talking with me." Serena stood and turned to the
circle. "Let's get up and stretch, then gather for the group photo."

Remi headed for the bathroom to ensure she wouldn't be in
the picture's background. Tuck followed her, as usual.

But Marta called him back. "Hey, Tuck, want a treat?" She stood by a table covered with snack food.

Doggo looked up for permission.

"Go ahead." Remi waved him on.

When she returned, the group had broken into clusters, and the reporter was talking to Marta, a recorder in one hand and a camera in the other. As Tuck trotted back to her side, Remi decided to leave. She waved at Gary, the only person looking her way, and headed out. Maybe coming here had been a mistake.

Chapter 14

The Recent Past
You're kinda in the background

Aug. 15, two weeks later (day 45 after the strike)

Remi opened a can of chili and stared at the brown lumpy goo. She was sick of this stuff, but she'd had about twenty cans in the cupboard. Which made no sense, unless she'd gotten it for free or had been stockpiling protein for the apocalypse. She looked down at Tuck. "I know you like it, so it's all yours." As she bent down to scrape some into his dish, a knock at the door startled her. She straightened up. Nobody ever came to her house. She was too far off the street even for salesmen and religious zealots.

Remi shuffled into the living room, thinking it must be Izzy. As she reached the door, a wave of fear washed over her. "Who is it?"

"Chris. I brought pizza."

Oh god. She wasn't ready to deal with strangers who seemed to know her. But the thought of hot pepperoni and melted cheese made her mouth water. She could smell it through the door. She glanced down at her clothes. Cargo shorts and a bleach-stained tank top. *Jeez.* If that wasn't sloppy enough, she wasn't wearing makeup and couldn't remember the last time she brushed her hair.

"Come on. You know you want it." The voice was so friendly, she ignored the possible sexual innuendo.

Hating herself, she pulled open the door. The person holding the pizza box was about five-ten, with shoulder-length sandy hair and a pleasant androgynous face. They also wore a baggy t-shirt and shorts. *Great.* She still didn't know if her friend was male or female. "Hi, Chris." Remi stepped aside and waved them in, inhaling the mouth-watering smell.

"Does that mean you remember me?" Chris grinned.

"No. Sorry. But you're here, and I appreciate that." A catch in her throat. "I've been kinda isolated." They'd been texting for weeks and even though Remi was sure they hadn't been hooking up, she'd been putting off this in-person moment.

Chris set the pizza on the coffee table and hugged her. "I hate what you're going through, and I hope I'm not making it worse."

"No. And thanks. I'm starving."

"Me too. Let's eat." Chris sat on the couch, and Tuck jumped into their lap.

Remi relaxed a little and sat on the other end. "Down boy. Not while we're eating."

Tuck gave her a look and trotted back to his own meal.

Chris opened the box, and they reached for slices at the same time. Remi smiled, feeling good about this person. Based on an earlier text, she knew they'd met at the daycare. "Where are you working now?"

"I'm doing in-home care for an elderly woman." Her friend made a face. "It's boring, so I've applied with the school district to be an assistant in their special-ed classes this fall."

"You're a nurturer."

Chris grinned. "Yep. Might as well get paid for it."

"Do you see *me* that way?" Her counselor's reference to *guilt* still haunted Remi, and she wondered what kind of person she really was.

"With kids, totally. You love them and they love you."

"I hope I can go back to work at the daycare."

"You still have pain?"

Remi started to make a joke, but couldn't. "All the time."

"I'm sorry."

They ate in silence for a while, then Chris said, "Hey, I saw the article about the group you're attending. I'm glad you found some support."

Remi's chest tightened. She'd been watching for the story online, but had somehow missed it. "Was my name used?"

"No. But the reporter quoted you anonymously."

Whew! "No photo either?"

"Nothing direct, but you're kinda in the background of a small photo of two other members hugging."

That didn't sound like a problem, but she wanted to see the whole thing. "Can I find the article online?"

Chris nodded, chewing a mouthful with a strong jaw. "What's the deal with not having your name or picture published?"

"I don't know." Remi put down her slice. "Did I ever tell you about my past? Before coming to Wilsonville?"

"I wish. But you wouldn't ever talk about it."

"Apparently, I told my counselor, but she won't fill me in." Remi sighed. "She wants me to remember on my own."

"I'm sure she has a good reason." Chris patted her leg.

The touch startled her. *How long had it been since she'd had physical contact with anyone?*

Remi reached for her laptop, which she kept close by, and quickly found the article. The group photo was cheesy, but seeing her new friends made her smile. She scanned the text and found her quote in the fourth paragraph after the reporter referred to "a woman, who now suffers with unusual memory conditions." But no mention of her name. *Perfect.* She wanted to print the story for safekeeping, but she didn't have a printer. Such an old-school idea anyway.

Remi ate another slice of pizza, then worked up her courage. "Can I ask an awkward question?"

"Sure. I'm as awkward as a person gets."

"What's your gender? I feel so stupid for not knowing."

Chris laughed. "I'm nonbinary, and you never cared about that."

"I still don't."

"Cool. Let's watch the latest episode of Handmaid's Tale. I've been saving it for this occasion."

Chapter 15

The Recent Past

An interesting connection to an old case

Aug. 15, Phoenix

Jamie Dallas flashed her badge at the security desk, then crossed the bureau's lobby to the bullpen where her desk sat among a dozen others. As an undercover FBI agent, she wasn't here enough to need an office. But she was currently between UC/travel assignments, so she was working fraud as her usual backup. White-collar crime and all its paperwork bored her, so she itched to get back into the field. Her boyfriend hated having her gone, but as an adrenaline junkie, she couldn't help but crave the excitement—and flexibility—of infiltrating criminal groups. Unfortunately, that wasn't on her schedule for today.

She booted up her computer and checked her emails. Mostly internal HR stuff, but the last one caught her attention. A Google alert for the name *Tuck*. She didn't remember setting it up, but he was probably a good ol' boy who'd been cooking meth in his trailer and blew himself up. Dallas sipped the coffee she'd picked up on the way and opened the message. A snippet of a news article displayed above a link, and she clicked the underline without reading the text.

A new page opened to a feature article in the *Portland Tribune* with the headline: *Support for Shock Survivors.* Displayed to the right was a large group photo.

What the hell?

Dallas scanned the text. No mention of anyone named Tuck, but still an interesting read. She hadn't known lightning strikes caused so much long-term damage to people's bodies, nerves, and brains. It shouldn't have surprised her. At least one Arizonan was killed by lightning every summer. But what did any of this have to do with her Google alert for Tuck? Who was he? She didn't remember a case with that name. Dallas focused on the photo to see if she recognized anyone. *No luck.* Below it was a smaller picture of a man with a metal prosthetic hugging an older woman. And behind them, a blurry shot of someone else. Dallas went back to the larger photo and read the tiny-print caption listing all their names. At the end, the text said: *Pictured below, Tuck.*

She scanned the bottom of the image and finally saw the dog. Tuck was a Jack Russell terrier. Now she remembered! A witness in a major fraud case had disappeared halfway through her testimony. The Tacoma taskforce she'd been working with assumed the woman had been threatened or bribed. They'd offered her witness protection soon after she'd confessed and entered a plea deal, but eventually the witness had gone AWOL.

After a quick search of digital files, Dallas opened the old case and skimmed through it. The crime ring had originally operated here in the Phoenix area, and she'd been assigned to join the police department's taskforce. The bureau had gotten involved because the suspected crimes had taken place in various towns around Phoenix, each with their own police department. That's how the crew had gotten away with the fraud for so long. By using various jurisdictions and insurance companies, they'd kept a pattern from emerging for years.

For her part in the case, Dallas had established an undercover persona and approached the ringleader's nephew, whom she'd assessed as the weakest member. But the family group had suddenly packed up and moved out, disappearing almost overnight. Without legal authority to pursue them, the Phoenix police had dropped their investigation. But the bureau had kept the family names and activities on their watch list, then eventually helped prosecute several members in the Seattle-Tacoma area. But their star witness, Riley Brockwell, had abruptly disappeared, and the patriarch, Aden Sebastiano, aka Yano, had walked away.

Brockwell had a dog named Tuck. And here was the same breed with the same name in Portland, Oregon, five hours south of their old stomping ground. *Coincidence?* Dallas didn't think so.

She clicked on the file image of Brockwell. Pretty, with dyed-blonde hair piled in a messy bun and heavy makeup, especially around her eyes. Dallas clicked back to the group shot in the news story and studied the faces again. All the women were twenty years too old, including the one in the smaller photo below. But someone in the group belonged with the dog and might know its previous owner.

She printed the file notes and called her boss.

"Special Agent Radner."

"Can I come up? I've got an interesting connection to an old case."

"I'll give you five minutes."

Dallas trotted up the stairs, already thinking about how she might find the witness or possibly go undercover to get close to Yano. She stepped into the corner office, the file in hand. Behind his desk, Radner hunched forward, masking the full size of his impressive frame. His gray curly hair, cut close to the scalp, contrasted with his dark skin, and he was gorgeous for an old guy. She found him sexually attractive, but she never used her feminine assets to get ahead in the bureau. She saved those for the bad guys, who couldn't seem to resist a pretty, young blonde.

"Agent Radner, thanks for your time."

"Five minutes. I have a call with the AD to prep for." He tapped a folder on his desk.

"Remember Aden Sebastiano?

"The gangster wannabe of insurance fraud? Oh yeah, he's unforgettable."

"I think the witness who went AWOL is in Portland, Oregon."

"So?" Her boss furrowed his forehead.

"What if I can get her to testify? Then into Witness Protection. You know Yano will never stop until we put him away."

A spark of interest in his eyes. "Did he come up on our watch list?"

"Not exactly." Dallas explained the alert she'd received.

"A dog?" Radner laughed. "If the witness was somehow connected to Yano, or if we could connect him to a current case…

"Can I spend some time on it?"

Radner chuckled again. "Five minutes."

"Oh come on. I'm wasted on this local charity fraud crap."

"I'll ask the AD if he has an undercover assignment for you. Until then, get back to work."

"Yes, sir."

Disappointed, Dallas headed back to her desk. She'd been looking forward to another trip to the northwest, where she'd conducted several important UC assignments. Anything to get out of Arizona's summer heat. But that was just an excuse. Yano was only one of two targets who'd gotten away with the crimes she'd been investigating. When the case against him had been dropped, the sick bastard had sent her an email, taunting her about the FBI's "failure," calling her and the taskforce "losers." This case not only felt personal, but Dallas sensed something was stirring. And she wanted to be part of the action.

Chapter 16

The Recent Past

What brings you here?

Aug. 17, Wilsonville (day 47 after the strike)

From her closet, Remi pulled out a summer dress with a flared skirt, tugged it on, and stared in her bedroom's full-length mirror. White wasn't a great color for her, but she loved the tiny pink blossoms with green leaves. She wanted to look nice for her second meeting with the group, yet still be comfortable. This would work.

"What do you think, Tuck?" He was on the bed watching her, expectant. He could tell she was getting ready to leave the house, which didn't happen often. She took the dress back off, put on a bra, which she only wore when she went out, then tugged the garment back over her head. It felt less comfy now, but looked better.

In the kitchen, she picked up the Aleve bottle she kept her stash in and transferred one tablet to the small Aleve bottle in her purse. She would take her second dose after the meeting and be home before it fully kicked in. She wanted to take it now, but would make herself wait. Remi swallowed a couple of the anti-inflammatories to hold off the pain until then.

Maybe she wouldn't go. The group offered emotional support, but they couldn't help with her memory loss and the pain of the drive was daunting. Remi headed back to the bedroom to change. As she kicked off her sandals, she caught site of herself in the mirror. *Oh hell.* She'd put on a damn dress. Might as well go out, see some people, and feel like a functioning member of society. Remi turned and started back up the hall. Tuck followed, nonjudgmental.

Later, in the grange parking lot, she almost changed her mind again. She'd already heard their personal stories. What else did they have to talk about? Oh yeah, they played cards, and according to Gary, danced sometimes. A shadowy image of herself swing dancing surfaced briefly. Was it a memory... or a projection? She didn't see herself ever being light enough on her feet to dance with a partner again.

She shut off her engine. "Okay. We're doing this."

Tuck wagged his tail, ready for anything.

Remi climbed out and a warm summer breeze lifted her skirt. The sensation was glorious, and for a moment she recalled a similar feeling while standing near a ferry. The memory faded quickly, but still, she felt encouraged. Inside the grange, she braced herself, then entered the meeting room. Seeing her new friends and their welcoming smiles lifted her heart again. This was why she'd come, despite her worries. These people understood her pain, her frustration with doctors, and her struggle to simply function most days. In the two weeks since her first group meeting, she'd felt better, or at least less depressed.

As she crossed to a chair, Gary whistled.

Remi blushed, glad she'd worn the dress. "Sorry I'm late again. The traffic is always worse than I expect." She took a seat, then blurted, "Actually, I changed my mind about attending several times."

"Why?" Alicia smiled warmly. "No more reporters, at least for a while."

"I'm not sure." Remi unleashed Tuck and stroked his head, feeling self-conscious. "I get so used to being alone at home that everything else seems like too much effort."

"We understand that." Alicia nodded. "I'm glad you're here."

"Me too." Gary grinned.

Remi noticed an empty chair and realized someone was missing. "Where's Doug?"

A heavy silence.

"He's in the hospital." Alicia's tone was somber. "One of his toes got infected and now he has sepsis. His immune system is weak from diabetes, which he developed after his strike."

"Oh no. He'll be all right, won't he?"

Alicia pressed her lips together. "We can only hope."

Remi glanced around. "How does everybody know about his hospitalization?" She felt left out somehow.

"We have a text chain," Marta cut in. "I thought you'd been invited to it."

Remi shook her head, too hurt to speak.

"I'm sorry. It was just an oversight."

Someone cleared their throat, and they all turned toward the door. A thirty-something guy stepped in. "Hi. I'm Thomas."

"Welcome," everyone said.

Remi couldn't help but stare as he walked over and took a seat. She loved his big eyes, wavy hair, and freckles. So her type.

He wore a sage-green t-shirt that didn't hide a bit of belly. A regular guy.

Alicia introduced each member, and when it was Remi's turn, Thomas beamed. "Cool. Like the champagne."

Remi smiled self-consciously. Had she chosen her first name too? After a drink? She didn't even like alcohol. "Nice to meet you."

"What brings you here?" Gary asked the newcomer, his tone guarded.

"I'm looking for support like the rest of you." Thomas blinked. "I got zapped while repairing a cell phone tower."

"You climb those?" Gary was wide-eyed.

"Not anymore." Thomas laughed and his whole face lit up. "I'm lucky to be alive."

"We're all lucky to be alive," Marta added.

Remi was glad she'd come. The new guy was a sweet addition to the group.

After the meeting, as they stood around eating cookies and discussing their Tribune feature, Thomas approached her. "Hey, are you going to the national conference?"

He'd sought her out! "I doubt it. The cost is out of my budget and I don't like to fly." That was news to her.

"Me neither." He took a bite of his Oreo.

Remi noticed little black tattoos on his fingers and tried not to be judgmental.

"I like your dog," Thomas said. "What's his name?"

"Tuck." Doggo was sniffing the man's shoes and wiggling his butt. "He likes you too."

"I passed the first test." Thomas grinned.

Flustered, Remi tried to think of a conversation starter. "How did you get into cell tower work?"

Thomas shrugged. "I kept seeing the job opening, so I figured no one else wanted the job and they'd be willing to hire me."

"They probably have a lot of turnover." Remi laughed. "And you aren't doing it anymore either."

"No. I hate heights." Another lovely smile. "I'm a bartender now. What about you?"

"I used to work at a daycare center."

He nodded. "You like kids."

Was that a statement or a question? "I do. And I hope to get back to work there someday, but I'm still recovering." She worried she was boring him. What else could she talk about?

He gestured toward her skirt. "I like your dress. Very summery."

"Thanks."

"Ever since I spotted you, I keep thinking you look familiar." Thomas tipped his head. "Have we met?"

She hoped so. "I don't know. I lost my memory after my lightning strike."

"That's awful." Thomas touched her arm.

A jolt of pleasure shot through her.

"I'll try to figure out where I might know you from," he added. "Maybe that will help."

"I'd like that." Remi smiled. He seemed so down to earth and easy to talk to.

Thomas handed her his phone. "Add your number and I'll text you if I think of it."

Butterflies danced in her heart. An attractive man wanted her contact information. This was either unexpectedly amazing… or a colossal mistake.

Chapter 17

The Recent Past
Her first date in… however long

Aug. 19 (day 49 after the strike)

Remi waited nervously in the Taco Loco parking lot. She'd
made an effort to be early for her lunch with Thomas, and
now he was late. What if he'd changed his mind? *Just stop,* she
coached herself. It was only two minutes after, and freeway traffic
was always unpredictable. He'd offered to pick her up, but out of
caution, she'd suggested a restaurant halfway between his location
in east Portland and her home in Wilsonville. Then she'd worried
about making the mid-day drive while medicated. But she'd built
up a tolerance to the methadone and it didn't affect her focus
anymore. She'd tried giving it up, but her headaches had come
back and without it, her butt pain made her limp and curse.
Some day she would wean off it, but not today. Not on her first
date in… however long.

An old black truck parked nearby and Thomas climbed out.
Remi watched him walk inside, still amazed that this handsome
guy wanted to date her. She petted Tuck. "Sorry you can't go in,
but I'll bring you a snack." He slumped into his disappointed-
but-resilient pose.

Remi strode inside, trying to walk normal and feel good about herself. She'd rushed out and bought the forest-green summer dress at a St. Vincent's right after Thomas had called, hoping the dark color would make her look slimmer. *It doesn't matter,* she reminded herself. It was just lunch. No expectations.

Remi stepped into the brightly painted lobby and Thomas was there, waiting for her. Points for that too. He'd texted her a few hours after the support-group meeting, saying: *I don't remember how I know you, but I'm sure that I want to. Can we get lunch in the next day or so?*

She'd been so giddy she'd wanted to text back: *Hell yeah!* But she'd made herself wait and respond with something more casual. Then he'd actually called, instead of texting, to arrange the details. Impressive.

"Ri—Remi." Another big smile.

He'd almost messed up her name, but she didn't care. They'd only met once. "Hi Thomas."

"You look so nice, I feel under-dressed." He wore khaki shorts and a black t-shirt that looked like it just came out of the package.

"You're fine," Remi soothed. "It's just tacos."

"*Just* tacos?" He feigned shock and disappointment. "Tacos are the bomb."

"I know. I chose this place."

"And in that moment, I liked you even more."

He liked her! "You haven't watched me eat yet."

They both laughed.

After studying the menu board, they ordered the same meal—a combo plate of beef tacos and black beans with salsa.

"I love anything with meat and cheese," Remi confessed. "And I hate most vegetables."

"Same here." Thomas made a face. "I'll eat salad if it has enough dressing and bacon."

Remi laughed. "And nothing else is offered." She dug in her purse for her wallet.

"I've got this." Thomas touched her forearm, then paid the counter person with cash.

They helped themselves to glasses of water, then he led her to a table near an open window. "This okay?"

A warm breeze caressed her skin as she sat across from a delightful man. "It's perfect."

Chapter 18

The Recent Past

Primitive impulses overrode her caution

Aug. 28, evening (day 58 after the strike)

Thomas shut off his engine. "I'll walk you to the door."

A surge of emotions paralyzed Remi. That meant he wanted to come in—and she wanted him to. This was their third date, and her body craved sex with him. But her brain kept saying no. She was too embarrassed about her pudge and freakish scars to get naked with anyone. The red spidery lines were fading a little, and she'd made a point to lose a few pounds, but it didn't change much. She was also terrified to open herself to that level of intimacy and bonding. She still didn't know anything about her past or why she lived like someone in hiding. It wouldn't be fair to Thomas to get deeply involved with him. What if her memory came back and it changed everything?

He was already climbing out of the truck, so she did too. *It was just sex*, she reminded herself.

At the front door, he lightly stroked her hair. "I love spending time with you."

The touch sent quivers down her body. But the word *love*

kind of freaked her out, even though he'd used it indirectly. Was his attention too much, too soon? That was always a red flag.

"I like you too." She started to tell him goodnight, but primitive impulses overrode her caution. "Would you like to come in?" She made an embarrassed sound in her throat. "Just to see my place." Mid-week they'd met for pizza and bowling—which she'd been surprisingly good at—but this date had been dinner and a movie. Thomas had originally asked her to go dancing, but she was still too awkward. This time, he'd insisted on picking her up, "like a gentleman."

"I'd love to."

That word again.

In the house, anxiety rolled around her head like a pinball. What should she do next? She didn't have any alcohol to offer. Or an art collection to show off. The thought made her laugh.

"What's funny?" Thomas reached for her and stepped in close.

"I was wishing I had an art collection to show you."

He smiled. "The only art I need is your lovely face."

Now he was scaring her. Remi stepped back.

"Hey, sorry. That was corny." Thomas laughed. "I told you I haven't dated in a while." He touched her shoulder this time. "I do think you're very pretty, but what matters is that I really like you."

"We hardly know each other." Still, on their second date, she'd surprised herself and told him about her fear and her counseling sessions.

"I know you're kind and funny. And you like the same food and streaming shows that I do."

Was that enough? "What if my memory comes back and I realize I'm not that person?"

"The past doesn't matter." Thomas leaned in and kissed her softly on the lips.

Remi's heart melted.

He pressed more urgently, and a tsunami of lust took over. She wanted his tongue, his body against hers, his cock inside her.

As he led her to the bedroom, she whispered, "I have scars."

"So do I."

"Not like mine."

Thomas turned on the bedroom light. "I want to see them, to see all of you."

Remi snapped the switch back off. "Not a chance. I'm chubby too."

"Don't say that. You are so sexy." He gently stroked her breasts.

Remi gave in and removed her shirt and bra. They eased onto the bed, and Thomas sucked her nipples and fingered her until she was so turned on she almost snapped at him to keep it moving.

"Do I have consent?" he whispered as he took off his pants.

"Yes."

When he was fully inside her, she cried out in pleasure, the feel and smell of his body intoxicating. But minutes later, a darkness descended, a grief and guilt so overwhelming she burst into tears. Thomas quickly extracted himself. "What's wrong? Did I hurt you?"

It took Remi a minute to get control. "No. I'm just overwhelmed. I guess it's been a while."

"We can wait." He lay beside her and pulled the sheet over them. "I've never made a woman cry during sex before."

"It's not you." *Or was it?* Something about him was emotionally powerful. Until this moment, she'd experienced those feelings as affection and longing. But now she felt lost, as though

he could never fully belong to her. None of it made sense. Unless…
Maybe this was about the methadone. She'd read that it could
suppress sex drive and orgasms, so it might be messing with her.
"I think you should go."

"Are you sure? I won't pressure you for sex, but I'd like to
stay."

Remi lay there, unable to make up her mind. She either had
to tell him about the drug or break it off. Finally, she confessed.
"I use methadone for my chronic pain."

"Whoa." Thomas sat up. "That's potent stuff."

"I know. I need to quit."

"Do you think it somehow made you cry?"

Remi rolled to look at him, and the poor guy was rubbing
his confused face.

"I don't know." Grief overwhelmed her again. "I'm just so sad
right now I think I should be alone."

"All right." He climbed out of bed and pulled on his pants.
"I'm not giving up." A pause. "Unless you want me to."

"Please don't."

The next day, Chris called, eager to know about her date. "Please
tell me you had sex."

"Not exactly." She didn't want to talk about it, but Chris had
been such a good friend, Remi felt obligated. "But sort of."

"What the hell does that mean?"

"We got going, and it was great, then I felt overwhelmed and
started crying."

"Oh shit, girl. You gotta get off the pain meds."

Remi had never told Chris what kind of medication she took. "I know."

"Did he freak out?"

"No. Thomas was great and still wants to see me."

"He sounds like a keeper."

Remi hesitated. "Yeah."

"What? Does he have a kinky fetish? Or an ugly tattoo on his ass?"

Remi gave a half-hearted laugh. She didn't know how to explain the grief and guilt that sex with Thomas had triggered, so she made light of Chris' remark. "No kinks, but he does have weird tattoos on his fingers."

Her friend's silence filled her with dread. "What? Does that mean something?"

"Yeah. He's been in prison."

Chapter 19

The Recent Past

Time to run again

Sept. 6 (the day before the kidnapping)

In a state of depression, Remi had ignored Thomas' texts for a week, then finally agreed to meet him at the taco place again "to talk it out." Now she sat across from him, sipping a watermelon slushy and sweating in the heat.

"Tell me what I can say or do to fix this," Thomas pleaded.

"Be honest about the tattoos on your fingers."

His shoulders slumped. "I planned to tell you, but there's never a good time to mention that you're an ex-con."

"What were you convicted of?"

"Fraud. It was a stupid scam with no real victims, except a greedy corporation."

Remi wanted to believe him. She'd called various state agencies trying to find information, but Thomas Downing hadn't been listed anywhere. "What prison were you in?"

"Coyote Creek in Washington state. I moved to Portland when I was released early this year." He reached across the table and grabbed her hands. "I'd never been in trouble before. But at the time, I'd lost my job and racked up some debts. Then someone I trusted pulled me into something that seemed like a harmless way to get back on track." Thomas hung his head. "I have such shame and regret."

"When were you gonna tell me?"

"Soon, I promise."

"But after we'd slept together."

He gave a sheepish smile. "I wanted to give our relationship a chance."

Remi wanted that too. And she had something in her past to feel guilty about, so she wasn't perfect either. "Okay. We'll try again."

"Thank you." Thomas beamed. "Now, will you order something to eat?"

Remi shook her head. "It's too hot, and I'm not really hungry." The methadone had that effect for the first couple of hours.

"Can I come over tomorrow tonight?"

A flutter of worry. "If you can take it slow. I don't want a repeat of last time."

"I'll let you set the pace." He squeezed her hands again. "I want to make you happy."

A little later, they stood in the parking lot saying goodbye with sweat dripping down their faces. "I have to get in my car and crank the air conditioning," Remi said.

"Good plan. I'll see you tomorrow around seven." Thomas leaned in, kissed her cheek, then jogged over to his truck. Before he climbed in, he pulled off his t-shirt. Remi stared at his tanned muscular torso. He'd been working in construction and obviously didn't wear a shirt on the job. The night they'd hooked up, she'd kept the lights off to hide her own body, so she hadn't really seen his. *Damn,* he looked good.

As he drove away, an odd thought occurred to her. For someone who'd suffered an electrical shock, he seemed quite unscathed. And he never talked about the incident or mentioned any pain or consequences.

Had he lied about it? But why would he?

Panic flooded her. Because he'd seen the article with the picture of Tuck and the smaller photo with her in the background? Then showed up to find her? *Oh fuck!* Remi started her car and sped toward the freeway. She tried to calm herself and be rational, but nothing worked to dissuade her. Thomas had done time in prison. He'd showed up at the meeting right after the article was published. He'd sought her out and pursued her until he found out where she lived. It all added up. She'd been lonely and gullible, and the amnesia had clearly eroded some of the protections she'd built around her life. It was time to run again.

Back at home, Remi took another pain tablet, knowing it would calm her anxiety, then started packing her clothes. A knock at the door made her heart pound. Was it Thomas? Of course not. He didn't know she'd caught on to him—and he had an invitation to come over tomorrow. Remi headed toward the door. "Who is it?"

"Chris."

The mid-afternoon visit was unexpected, but Chris was the one person she trusted. Remi pulled open the door. Her friend's eyes were puffy and stressed from previously shed tears.

"What's going on?" Remi stepped back and waved Chris in.

"Jordan had a meltdown, then we had a big fight. Can I stay here for a day or two? Just to get some space?"

Remi forced herself to nod and smile. "Sure." Yesterday, she would have been glad for the company. But everything had changed, and now she needed to get away from this house, this town—while she still could. Her rent was paid for the month, and she could leave anytime, then text her landlord as she drove away.

But not today. Her friend needed her for a few days. Plus she had a counseling appointment scheduled for tomorrow. Might as well try one more time to jumpstart her memory. She would text Thomas in the morning to break their date, then tell him she wanted to reschedule. No reason to tip him off that she'd figured out his game. Meanwhile, she would start packing and figure out where to go next.

Remi closed the door and smiled at Chris. "Let's order pizza."

Chapter 20

The Turbulent Present

A one-woman special op

Sept. 8, Phoenix (the day after the kidnapping)

Dallas hit the ground hard, then ran to a stop. For a full minute, she stood in the field, savoring the high-flying body joy of another parachute jump. She loved these early morning adventures before heading to work. She had so many vacation days built up, her boss encouraged her to use a half day every once in a while. As she jogged back to the airstrip and hangar, she hoped the adrenaline fix would hold her over. What she really needed was an undercover case that would give her a steady stream of juice. She loved taking on a new persona and walking right into a criminal lair. The best acting gig imaginable. She'd been getting those assignments regularly for years, but now she'd been stuck in the bureau for months. A depressing thought crept in. She'd just turned thirty, so her young-sexy-blonde appeal might be fading enough that the bureau had bumped her from that special UC list. *Shit.* Dallas shook it off and tried to recapture the joy she'd felt a moment ago. Her body was still humming, but her brain had already locked into work mode.

Late that afternoon at her desk in the Phoenix bureau, she checked her email. Another alert for the word *Tuck*. Dallas' pulse quickened. She clicked the link and the connection took her to a second newspaper story in the *Oregonian*. The headline was disturbing: *Wilsonville Woman Goes Missing.*

Dallas skimmed the brief article: *Wilsonville resident Remi Bartel (31) disappeared Thursday after an appointment with a counselor, and her roommate reported her missing when she didn't come home that night. Bartel and her dog, Tuck, a Jack Russell terrier, were recently featured in an Oregonian story about a support group for victims of lightning strikes. A spokesperson for the Wilsonville Police said they don't suspect foul play because Bartel's vehicle had not turned up, and like most people reported missing, she probably traveled somewhere without notifying anyone. The spokesperson also said they would welcome the public's help in finding her. If you know Bartel or have any information about her location, please contact the department.*

Another short paragraph summarized the earlier feature, but no photo accompanied the news brief. Highly unusual. Dallas jumped to her feet and charged upstairs to Radner's office. The door was closed, meaning someone was in there. *Damn.* She hurried back down to her desk.

"What's up with you?" her cube neighbor asked, rolling his chair closer.

"An old case with loose threads that have started to unravel."

"And you want to go after it." He flipped her the finger. "I'm sure the boss will let you."

Dallas gave him a *who-me?* look, then went back to her computer. She searched for the number of the Wilsonville police and made the call. "FBI Agent Jamie Dallas. I need to speak to the officer handling the Bartel disappearance."

"He's not available." The desk officer sounded busy. "I can pass along your number though."

Dallas rattled it off. "Please send me the missing-persons report and any other information you have on Bartel."

"Can I ask why the FBI is interested?"

"Bartel might be part of an open case." Dallas rolled her eyes. "And in danger."

"Give me your email, and I'll send the file."

After hanging up, Dallas texted her boss: *I need to see you ASAP!*

While waiting for the police report and invite upstairs, she checked Facebook and Instagram for Remi Bartel. Not one single hit. Dallas ran an open Google search and found nothing. The woman was either a Luddite—unheard of for a millennial—or in hiding. Dallas opened the original news story in the *Oregonian*. Remi Bartel hadn't been named or photographed, but there was a quote from an anonymous member. After being hit by lightning, the woman had lost her memory, but had gained a new ability to recall anything she read or heard. Also unusual, but not likely important to her disappearance. No specific mention of whether the dog named Tuck was hers.

Dallas scrolled to the smaller picture and zoomed in on the face in the background. The image was blurry, but likely female, with light-brown hair and a little heavier than Brockwell. If their witness had gained weight and stopped dying her hair...

The police report came in moments later and Dallas skimmed it. Nothing new except the missing woman's address and the name of the roommate who'd filed the report. The small-town department was probably overworked and not giving the case much attention. Thousands of missing-person reports were filed every day and most of the subjects turned up on their own. Unless there was blood or signs of a struggle, standard law enforcement response was to wait a few days before wasting resources. If Remi Bartel was in fact their witness, Riley Brockwell, she didn't have a few days. In all likelihood, she was already dead. But if Yano had kidnapped or killed her, Dallas might be able to gather enough evidence to finally put him away. She got up to pace.

A moment later, she headed upstairs again. This couldn't wait.

She nodded at an agent leaving the corner office, then stood in Radner's doorway. Her phone pinged in her hand, and her boss looked up and laughed. "What's so urgent?"

Dallas stepped inside, but didn't sit. "Remember the old case I mentioned a couple weeks ago? The dog named Tuck?"

"Barely. Why?"

"His owner disappeared yesterday." Dallas bounced on her feet. "Her name is Remi Bartel and she has no social media presence."

"Remind me why we care." Dry with a chance of sarcasm.

"Aden Sebastiano, aka, Yano."

"Oh right. The witness who went AWOL and blew our case against him."

"Her name was Riley Brockwell and she had a dog named Tuck. The missing woman is Remi Bartel and she has a dog named Tuck."

A moment of silence.

"Yano found her." Radner's tone was solemn this time.

"I know. She's likely dead. But what if she isn't?" Dallas started to pace. "Either way, this could be our chance to nail him. Six million in insurance fraud that we know of. Plus other suspected side hustles." She would dig back into those when she had time.

"And you want to follow up in person?"

"Of course, sir."

"You'll need to work with the local police."

That was a yes! "I already have their initial report."

"Where's our nearest field office?"

"Portland, Oregon."

"I'll get them on board with a contact person for you." Radner gave her a look. "Don't be a one-woman special op."

Dallas laughed. "Believe me, if I find Yano, I'll call for backup."

At home in her condo, Dallas pulled out her carry-on travel bag, then stared into her closet. This trip was challenging to pack for because she didn't have a set persona and didn't know what to expect. She'd bought a ticket in her own name, which she rarely did, and needed professional clothes for dealing with local law enforcement. But if she located Yano, she might need to go undercover. No big deal. The bureau could create fake ID on short notice, and she could buy whatever she needed. She packed her favorite clothes, then made the call she'd been dreading.

Cameron didn't pick up but texted her a few minutes later: *Busy at work. What's up?*

He owned a brewing company and tavern in Flagstaff, 140 miles north of Phoenix, where they'd gone to high school together. They'd reconnected a year and a half ago when she'd gone home for her father's funeral. Their relationship was relegated to long weekends and short vacations, and she was content with that. Cameron wasn't.

Dallas keyed in a message, then deleted it. This conversation deserved a phone call. But she had a flight to make and didn't want to wait until she was at the airport. Cameron deserved better. She tried again: *I'm flying out to Portland tonight on a new assignment. Sorry to miss our weekend!*

She headed to the bathroom to pack the rest of her essentials, then sat down to search for a decent motel in Wilsonville. A message from Cameron displayed on her laptop: *Undercover? I won't hear from you?*

Dallas texted: *No. Just an old case. I'll probably be back in less than a week.*

Cameron: *Relieved! But I'll miss you.*

Dallas: *Call me when you have time.*

She made a room reservation, then checked her packing list. *Oh yeah.* She pulled her Glock from its locked case and tucked it into a compartment in her luggage. One of the benefits of being in law enforcement. After a moment, she grabbed her little Saturday Night Special and the purse with the hidden compartment… just in case.

Chapter 21

The Turbulent Present
This dude was batshit crazy

Sept. 9, Portland (day 2 after the kidnapping)

Remi crossed the garage and climbed into the back of the van, leaving the B&B rental the same way she'd entered. At least this time, only her wrists were bound. No tape on her mouth and no bag over her head. Apparently, Blake had started to trust her a little. Or maybe now that she'd been financially useful, they didn't care what she saw, which meant Yano intended to kill her.

Without the use of her hands, she collapsed awkwardly to the hard metal floor and grimaced in pain. She leaned back against the side wall, feeling like shit and desperate for a shower. After they'd shoved her into the storage room last night, she'd changed out of the waitress clothes and back into her tank top and cargo shorts just to be comfortable. The paring knife was in a side pocket and pressing into her upper leg.

Blake climbed in behind her and eased into the cushioned swivel seat that looked like it had been torn out of an RV. He set Tuck's cage on the floor beside him and Remi tried to smile at her boy. He didn't seem as drugged, but poor doggo had to be confused and stressed. She heard the garage's overhead door open, then Seth jumped into the driver's seat and started the engine. As they rolled out into the bright sunshine, Remi promptly vomited.

"What the fuck?" Blake jerked forward, looking like he might hit her.

"Sorry. I can't help it."

Seth stopped at the street, then started to pull out.

"What are ya doin'?" Blake yelled. "We gotta clean this up. I'm not riding with that smell."

Seth slammed the brakes and backed up the driveway. "We don't have the remote door opener anymore."

"Fuck. I left the key inside too." Blake rummaged through an empty fast-food bag and pulled out some napkins. He shoved them into Remi's bound hands. "Clean it up."

She did the best she could.

Blake held out the paper sack for her to drop the soggy mess into, then opened the sliding door and tossed the bag. "I need some air." He stepped out of the van, then spun back to question her. "Why are you puking? Are you pregnant?"

Remi almost laughed. "Maybe it was motion sickness."

"You didn't puke on the drive here."

Seth got out and joined Blake at the side door, hands deep in his jean pockets and shoulders hunched. "Maybe she's detoxing."

"From what?" Blake scowled, looking back and forth between them.

"Methadone." Remi started to shake. "I was in a lot of pain after the lightning strike. I still am."

"I have some Vicodin she can take," Seth casually suggested.

Blake spun toward the driver. "You knew about this and didn't tell me."

"I didn't think it was a big deal."

Blake punched him in the chest. "Keepin' stuff from me is bullshit!"

Seth gulped for air and rubbed his heart.

"So give her the damn Vicodin," Blake commanded. "We need to get on the road."

Seth dug in a duffle bag, then handed her a single tablet and a bottle of water.

"Just one?" Remi knew it wasn't enough to control either her pain or her withdrawals.

"Time to kick the habit. But I'll ease you down."

She swallowed the pill and gulped extra water. She'd had nothing to eat or drink this morning and only two sandwiches the whole day before. But no one had hit her in the face yet today.

The men climbed back in the van and they pulled out again. Neither thug had mentioned where they were going, but Remi assumed they were headed north into Washington. She'd heard Seth mention Tacoma once, and she knew it was just south of Seattle. No memories of the area had surfaced, but Remi was sure she'd been there at some point. It wasn't a good feeling.

Once they were out of town and on the freeway, Seth pushed the old van until it felt like they were doing eighty. The engine whined as they weaved in and out of traffic, passing cars on the right and left. Wanting to be anywhere else in the world, Remi closed her eyes and imagined herself on the beach with Tuck, playing in the ocean and enjoying the breeze. She wished she could hold him or even touch him through the wire cage. Days without his physical love and energy left her feeling hollow.

"Can Tuck sit in my lap for a while? I got you a great financial tip, right?"

Blake grunted. "You got booted from the dinner early, so who knows what you missed. Don't ask again."

Her poor baby. What if he thought she'd done this to him? Or didn't care about him anymore? "Hey, Tuck," she called softly. "You're a good boy. I love you."

"Oh, spare me." Blake reached over and pinched her mouth. "Shut the fuck up."

Remi took long slow breaths to keep from kicking him in the face.

Ten minutes later, Seth swore and let off the gas. "We got a cop on our tail."

The wail of a distant siren grew quickly louder.

"Fuck." Blake snapped his head toward the tinted back window. "How fast were you goin'?"

"Only seventy something," Seth mumbled.

Remi glanced out the rear glass and saw flashing red and blue lights gaining on them. *Please let him pull us over.*

The big guy abruptly grabbed her shoulder and yanked. "Get down and lay flat.

As she stretched out her legs to comply, Blake grabbed Tuck's cage and moved it near the front, then punched Seth's arm. "The dog is sick and you're takin' him to the vet. That's why you were speeding. And I'm nappin'. If he asks."

The lights and siren were right behind them now. Seth braked and eased off the road.

The big guy threw a jacket over Remi's face, then lay on top of her. His weight was crushing, and her sliver of hope died as she struggled to breathe. Taking labored, shallow breaths, she only half heard the conversation between Seth and the officer. But the stop was over too quickly for him to have been ticketed.

When they were back on the road at a slower speed, Blake finally rolled off and moved the jacket. Remi gasped and sucked in oxygen, but her reprieve was short lived.

"What the hell is in your pocket?" Blake grabbed at her shorts and yanked out the knife. "You little bitch!" He leaned over, his nasty breath hot on her face. "You were gonna stick me with this?" He held the blade against her cheek. "This little thing?" The big guy laughed, a heinous sound. "This wouldn't even have slowed me down. But you? I could kill and carve you with this."

She held perfectly still, hoping he wouldn't cut her face.

Tuck whined, and Blake grabbed his cage and shook it. "Both of you, shut the fuck up." He tossed the knife into a duffle bag and sat back in his captain's chair. "Just lay there quietly and I won't have to tape your mouth again."

Remi complied. What choice did she have?

An hour or so later, they surprised her and took an early exit. She tried to visualize where they were, but she wasn't familiar with southern Washington. But she knew most of the area between Vancouver and Tacoma was rinky-dink and rural. She wanted to sit up and watch where they went, but she didn't dare ask. The van moved slowly, stopping twice at what she assumed were traffic lights, then pulled into an area that smelled like deep-fried food. *Yes!* She was starving.

They spent a few minutes at a drive-up window where Seth ordered cheeseburgers and fries. When they were on the road again, Blake kicked her. "Get up."

Remi pulled herself upright, straining her weak stomach muscles.

He handed her a burger. "Eat this before we get there."

Using zip-tied hands, she wolfed half, then held out the rest. "For Tuck."

Blake rolled his eyes. "Bread isn't good for him." But he pulled out the meat and gave it to doggo, then handed the soggy bun back to her. Remi ate it quickly, not knowing when they would feed her again. Now that she was upright, she looked out the front and back windows, trying to determine their location. They soon passed a sign that said *Toledo,* wherever the hell that was.

The van picked up speed for a few miles, moving past a suburb with new homes into an area with fields and farms. They slowed again and turned left off the road, then rolled down a long driveway and stopped. A black metal gate stood in their path. Seth climbed out and punched a code into a security box, and they were soon parked in front of a gaudy mini-mansion. Two levels of fake-rock exterior, tall narrow glass, and ornate flourishes, including a portico supported by Roman-style columns that looked added on. The home of someone who wanted to look rich, but probably wasn't. Remi didn't sense that she'd ever been here, but dread filled every cell of her body.

"Let's go," Blake commanded. He stood outside the open van door, holding Tuck's cage.

Remi processed the words, but felt paralyzed.

The big guy grabbed her by the zip-tie and yanked her forward. She landed on her knees and cried out.

"Don't make me drag you."

Feeling queasy, she crawled to the opening and eased her legs out and down to the asphalt. A moment later, she vomited the cheeseburger.

"Oh fuck. Enough with the puking!" Blake turned to the driver. "Give her another Vicodin. I don't want this shit in front of Yano. He'll blame me."

Remi desperately wanted the drug—for so many reasons—but she hated her own weakness. Still, fighting an addiction on her way to be executed wasn't in her level of self-discipline. She gulped down the tablet with the last swallow from her water bottle and looked around. The property, about a half-acre, was surrounded by a tall metal fence. Even if she had the nerve to run, she was trapped.

As they approached the house, the garish-red double doors opened, and a man stepped out. Around six feet tall, dressed in a black track suit, with a muscular chest and a middle-aged belly. His red sneakers matched the door, and his dyed strawberry-blond hair was combed over a bald patch.

"Riley!" he boomed with a friendly callout.

Remi's knees buckled. She knew this voice, and it was deceptively dangerous.

Blake grabbed her arm and propelled her forward.

"Come on in." Yano pulled his lips back but it wasn't a smile. "After you." He stepped aside, and Remi forced herself to enter. Three men, all with quick fists, surrounded her. Compliance was her only option. She glanced over at Tuck, still in his carried cage, and felt sick at what they might do to him.

"Let's take this into my office." Yano strode past them and headed to the back of the house.

Remi followed down the hall. What was she willing to do to save herself? Not much. To save her dog? Almost anything. The thought of what that might be sickened her.

Moments later, Blake shoved her down into a padded chair

in a dark man-cave office. Three feet away, Yano leaned against the front of a large desk. Tuck's cage was on the floor next to him. Blake stayed at her side, and Seth stood near the door. Remi's heart pounded so hard she thought she was having a heart attack.

"I hear you don't remember me." Yano stuck a piece of gum in his mouth. "I don't believe it. Nobody ever forgets me."

Remi's throat was too dry to speak.

"Did you also conveniently forget what you did to me?"

Remi nodded. "I'm sorry." Her dry throat tickled and she coughed. "Can I have some water?" She was afraid to throw up again.

Yano laughed, a brief unnatural sound. "This aint a fuckin' service bar."

Blake snapped at Seth to fetch bottled water from the kitchen. He apparently didn't want her vomiting either.

"Let me remind you of a few things," Yano said, stepping toward her, chewing aggressively. "You cost me millions." A cold deadpan voice, followed by a fist smashed into her face.

The pain stunned her and blood trickled from her nose.

"Get up before you ruin my chair."

Rage took over and Remi bolted upright, hands clenched.

"You put my wife in prison." He slammed a fist into her gut. *Oh god.* She doubled over, fighting the urge to puke.

"And you took my son." Another punch, this one to her chest.

Gasping for air, Remi hoped she would pass out. Yano abruptly lurched toward her. Remi braced, but the blow didn't come. Track-suit man threw his arms around her and squeezed her in a paralyzing hug.

"I'm sorry to hurt you, Riley, but I had to. Because you hurt me." Another squeeze. "I still love you." He kissed her forehead.

"That Genovics stock tip you picked up is already a winner." Just as quickly, he let go, grabbed a tissue from his desk, and handed it to her. "Wipe your face and stop sniveling. We have work to do."

Stunned and shaking, Remi dabbed at her nose. This dude was batshit crazy.

Chapter 22

The Turbulent Present
Thank god someone gives a shit

Sept. 9, Wilsonville (day 2 after the kidnapping)

Dallas opened her eyes and, for a moment, didn't know where she was. She sat up, drawn to the window where beams of sunlight snuck in around the edges of the dark curtain. *Oh right.* A motel in Podunk, Oregon. Eager to start her investigation, she climbed out of bed, still groggy from a late flight arrival into the Portland airport, followed by a midnight drive south in a rental car.

She brewed a cup of hotel coffee, took a shower, and dressed in slacks and a sleeveless blouse. Even here, it was still too hot in the afternoons to wear layers, but she would take a blazer with her for when she needed to look professional or deal with excessive air conditioning. Her first stop would be the police department. After that, she hoped to search the missing woman's house.

As she climbed into the Kia Soul she'd rented, Dallas changed her mind and headed straight for the victim's home. She would check in with the local cops later. She already had their report and didn't want to deal with turf animosities or roadblocks before she even started.

Six minutes later, she found the address at the end of a dead-end street and knocked on the old farmhouse door. An older woman with a gray afro answered. "What do you want?"

"Agent Dallas, FBI. I'm looking for Remi Bartel. Who are you?"

"Izzy Johnson, her landlord."

Not the name of the roommate who'd filed the missing-persons report. "But Remi lives here?"

"She's in the back. Or she was." The old woman opened the screen door and stepped out. "What's your interest in Remi?"

"She's likely in danger, and I would appreciate whatever you can tell me about her." Dallas kept her voice deadpan. "Especially anything odd that might have happened in the last few days."

"Let me grab my tea, and we'll sit out here to talk. Want some?"

"No thanks." She watched the woman slip back inside and wondered what she had to hide.

When Izzy returned, she handed Dallas a glass of ice water. "It would be rude to not serve you something."

Dallas took a sip and sat in one of the ratty porch chairs. "How long has Remi been your tenant?"

"Two years.

About the time Riley Brockwell disappeared.

"I might as well tell you"—Izzy lowered her voice—"Remi paid me upfront in cash if I would rent to her without signing a contract."

Like a person in hiding. "Did Remi tell you anything about her past?"

"Nope." The old woman slurped her tea. "You know she recently lost her memory after getting' hit by lightning? She was in a lot of pain. Her burns were so bad. Poor thing."

Whole new scenarios opened up. "Do you think Remi might have killed herself?"

Izzy shrugged. "Probably not. She was getting better."

"Did anything unusual happen recently?"

A hesitation. "She started dating some guy who drove a truck."

Maybe interesting. "Do you know his name?"

"Nope."

Dallas stood, ready to see Bartel's home. "Will you let me into her place?"

"A friend of hers is staying over for a few days, and I think he's there now."

Dallas drove to the rear house, which wasn't visible from the street. A secluded cottage, cash payments, no social media presence. Remi Bartel had totally kept to herself—except for someone she started dating right before she disappeared.

The person who answered the door was a couple inches taller than Dallas with shoulder-length hair, a pink skirt, and an Adam's apple. Dallas shifted into nongender thinking and introduced herself.

The roommate shook her hand. "Chris Folsom. Are you here about Remi?"

Dallas nodded.

"Thank god someone gives a shit." Chris waved her in. "The police haven't even been here. They took my report and said she would probably turn up on her own." Chris rolled their eyes. "So I called the reporter at the Oregonian and asked her to run another news piece. But I couldn't even find a picture of Remi to send her."

"It's good that you contacted the paper. That's how I got involved." Dallas stepped inside and reminded herself that Chris was a suspect too. "Where did you two meet?"

"At KinderCare. We both worked there at the time."

"But you don't live here?" Dallas looked around. The place was tidy and minimalistic.

"No. I had a fight with my partner and needed to cool off." Chris glanced at their phone. "But I'm going home soon."

"I'd like to ask you questions as I look around."

"Perfect. I'll follow and try to be helpful."

In the living room, Dallas opened the end-table drawers and found nail clippers, batteries, and tissues. "When did you see Remi last?"

"Thursday afternoon. Remi said she had a counseling appointment and left, then never came home."

Almost forty-eight hours. That didn't bode well for the missing woman. "What does she drive?" Dallas stuck her hands in the crevices of the recliner and came out with popcorn.

"An old green Mazda. The police said they would put out a BOLO for it."

Maybe Remi/Riley had simply gone AWOL again. "Do you know her counselor's name?" Dallas assumed the therapist wouldn't tell her anything without a subpoena, but she had to ask.

"Remi mentioned the name Joanne, so I searched online and figured it has to be Joanne Whitmer. Wilsonville only has five counseling offices."

"Thanks. That saves me time." Dallas headed for the hall. "I need to see Remi's bedroom."

"To the left."

The door was open. Another minimalist space with only a bed, dresser, and nightstand. A suitcase was open on the bed with a pair of jeans and a sweater inside, as though Remi had started to pack, then been interrupted. Dallas turned to Chris. "Was she planning a trip?"

"Not that I know of."

Had Bartel gotten spooked and run without her personal things? Dallas strode to the closet and pulled out a second piece of luggage. Empty. Behind it, she found a small metal safe on wheels. Not a typical household item. She dragged it out into the room. "I don't suppose you know the combination?"

Chris shook their head.

"Do you know Remi's birthday?"

"Wow." A wide-eyed look. "I don't. That's weird, huh?"

"Not if she's who I think she is."

"Remi's not her real name?"

"Probably not." Dallas decided to take the safe with her and try a few combinations later tonight. Most people weren't creative with codes or passwords, and she'd guessed a few computer accesses in her UC work.

"You think she's in danger, don't you?" Chris looked upset for the first time.

"Most likely." Dallas pushed the safe toward the hall. "Tell me about Remi's new boyfriend."

"His name's Thomas, and she met him at the support group. That's all I know."

"Did you meet him?"

"No."

The new couple had probably been texting. "Is Remi's phone in the house somewhere?"

Another head shake. "I looked. And I've tried contacting her and gotten no response."

Dallas rolled the safe to the living room, then turned back to the hall. She opened a door into a laundry area and spotted a dog entry. "Tuck. Where is he?"

"I'm sure he's with Remi. She took him everywhere."

Dallas checked the bathroom, didn't find any medications, then moved to the guest room. The narrow bed had a blanket wadded on top and a small overnight bag on the floor nearby.

"I've been sleeping in here," Chris said from behind her.

Dallas spotted a stack of boxes in the corner and stepped over. They were all empty retail boxes. *Huh.*

"Do you need anything else from me?" Chris asked. "I have to go home."

"I'm good for now, but give me your number." As Chris recited it, Dallas keyed the info into her phone.

"Text me if you need anything." Chris grabbed the overnight bag off the floor and headed out.

Dallas decided to visit the counselor, then pick up her luggage from the motel. It made more sense to just stay here as her home base than to drag the heavy safe to her motel room. And she fully intended to get it open. Figuring out what people were hiding was her specialty.

Chapter 23

The Turbulent Present

Feeling like an intruder

Twenty minutes later

Following GPS directions, she pulled into a corner lot with an old, boxy two-story building. Based on the tacky signs, the counselor had a solo practice on the second level, which she shared with a massage therapist. A computer-repair business took up the ground floor. The five slots in front were filled, so Dallas drove to the back. As she climbed out, she scanned the small parking lot. No green Mazda. The police report hadn't mentioned the vehicle, so she wasn't surprised. And, she reminded herself, it was possible Remi/Riley had simply left town in a hurry. The adjacent lot was undeveloped, and beyond it was a city park with clusters of oak and fir trees. Dallas tossed her blazer back in the Kia. It was already too warm to even carry it.

As she started toward the building, a middle-aged woman in a pale-gray dress came down the exterior staircase. Dallas jogged over to intercept her. "Joanne Whitmer?"

The woman stopped, squinting in the morning sun. "Yes."

"Agent Dallas, FBI. I'm looking for Remi Bartel."

"Is she in trouble? Is that why the police called me?" The counselor looked distressed. "I haven't returned their call yet."

"She might be in danger." Dallas showed her badge, something she rarely did. "Did Remi keep her appointment yesterday?"

"Yes. But I can't tell you anything we discussed."

Dallas asked anyway. "Did Remi talk about leaving town?"

"No." Whitmer pressed her lips together. "You'll need to get a subpoena for any personal information."

"You were the last person to see her. Can you at least help with logistics?"

"Maybe." She shifted her purse strap higher on her shoulder. "I don't have much time. I was only going to my car between appointments to get a phone charger."

"Just a few non-personal questions. What was Remi wearing?"

"Black shorts and a bright green tank top."

A car pulled in nearby, and they stepped over to the building's walkway.

"What about her vehicle?" Dallas pressed. "Did Remi drive here?"

Whitmer frowned. "You know what's odd? I left here late that day, and the only other car in the lot was a dark-green compact, like a Honda or something. And I remember thinking it was probably Remi's car. I'm not sure why I knew that, but I was surprised it was still here."

A nerve pinged at the top of Dallas' spine. "But she wasn't in it."

"No. I thought Remi might have gone to the park for a walk." She gestured at the nearby greenery.

"Did you see the car again?"

The counselor shook her head. "It was gone yesterday morning when I arrived, and I assumed the computer guy had it towed. He hates the overnight party campers."

"What company?"

Whitmer pointed to a sign posted by Tidewater Towing.

Dallas keyed the number into her phone. The vehicle was probably a dead end, but now she knew Remi had likely disappeared from this parking lot. "Anything else you can tell me?"

"No. But I hope you find her."

Dallas nodded. Yet the scenario that played in her mind was Yano's grunts pushing Remi's car into a river with her in the trunk. Dallas scanned the back of the building. "Are there security cameras?"

"No. But now I wish there was." Whitmer abruptly started toward the stairs. "I have a client soon."

Back in her rental Kia, Dallas turned on the air conditioning, then called the tow company. After five rings, the call went to voicemail and a grumpy-sounding guy said, "I'm outside workin'. Leave a message and I'll get back to you."

She considered hanging up and driving over—it couldn't be far in this dinky town—but if the guy was out towing a vehicle, her time would be wasted. Or he might be one of those people who didn't answer calls from non-local area codes. Remi's car was a lower priority than her locked safe, so she left a message: "This is Jamie Dallas, and I need information about the green Mazda you picked up two nights ago. Please call me." She repeated her number twice just for clarity. Gut instinct had cautioned her not to specifically mention the FBI.

Not feeling optimistic about hearing from Grumpy Guy, she headed for her motel.

An hour later, Dallas set her luggage down in the victim's home, feeling like an intruder. She rationalized her presence by assuming the missing woman was either dead or would want to be found. Stomach growling, she headed to the kitchen to eat the chicken sandwich she'd picked up. She'd also taken a quick swim in the motel's pool to cool off. The northwest heat surprised her. The other occasions she'd been to Oregon had been quite pleasant. This time, she'd overheard locals complaining that the weather was "bipolar, raining one day and scorching the next."

Still hungry, Dallas checked the fridge. Eggs, cheese, and a bag of apples. Perfect for breakfast too. Munching one of the apples, she opened kitchen drawers, scanning for anything informative. In the junk drawer on the end, with the usual assortment of rubber bands and promotional pens, she found a key fob. A spare for the Mazda? Dallas slipped it into a pocket of her blazer. The key might come in handy when she visited the tow yard in the morning.

A bottle of Aleve next to the toaster caught her attention. The landlord had mentioned Remi's chronic pain, so Dallas was curious to know how she'd been treating it. She popped off the cap and was surprised to see the pills were squarish and peach-colored, not blue and oval like they should be. What had Remi been taking? Dallas dumped one into her hand and examined it closely.

The front was stamped with *M2540*, and the backside had a four-quadrant score, meant for cutting the pills into smaller chunks. The M likely stood for the manufacturer and the numbers referred to dosage. She went to the living room, dug out her laptop, and googled the description. Mallinckrodt, 40 milligrams of methadone. *Holy shit.* That was a lot of opioid. The fact that the pills weren't in a prescription bottle meant Remi had likely bought them on the black market. Illegal and dangerous. Had the woman gotten involved with new criminals? Dallas felt discouraged. The drug use meant Bartel might not be a good witness even if she could find her.

Still, Dallas was determined to learn, one way or another, if Bartel and Brockwell were the same person. The safe sat right there on the floor in front of her, so she decided to tackle it next. She would work at the combination for a while, then get up and search intermittently to keep from getting frustrated or bored. She scooted off the couch down to the floor and scraped her back on something hard. A laptop protruded from under a cushion. *Yes!* It might be a better place to start. Sometimes a browser history revealed a lot about a person.

The computer was a complete bust. Bartel had almost no files. The two exceptions being recipes and photos of her dog. Her browser history was equally uninformative, with most of her searches related to the support group and medical articles about how to treat burns and chronic pain. Dallas wondered if, before the lightning strike, Bartel had deleted all her searches. That kind of behavior indicated paranoia, which could be either a mental illness or a necessary survival mode.

Now for the safe. Dallas checked her own files for Rockwell's birthday and tried a few variations. No luck. With nothing else to go on, she googled an alphabet/number code and tried Remi's four-letter name. Nope. She used it backward with no success either. What else would be familiar and important to the woman? Oh yeah, her dog. Dallas tried Tuck, spelled forward, then backward. The lock clicked. Almost too easy. She pulled open the thick metal door and let out a whistle. That was a lot of cash for an unemployed daycare worker. She picked up a stack, pulled off the band, and rifled through it. All hundreds. But it wasn't a large safe, so maybe thirty thousand at the most. Had Brockwell stolen it from Yano? Maybe that was why she'd been hiding and he'd come after her.

Dallas took photos of the money, then carefully counted it. Twenty thousand, four hundred and fifty. She picked up her laptop, wrote a report, then emailed the documentation to her boss. She started to return the cash, then checked the back of the safe to make sure she hadn't missed anything. A key was tucked into the corner. Keeping a key in a safe meant it was too important to misplace. Her best guess was a safe-deposit box. But where?

Legs cramping, Dallas got to her feet and decided to go out for a run before the sun set. She downed a glass of water, then stepped outside to check the temperature. It had cooled to a lovely seventy or so with a nice breeze, and the sun was dropping in a gorgeous pink sky. Her favorite time of day.

On the road out front, she heard a big engine slow down and pull into the driveway.

Dallas jogged over to get a look. The driver spotted her, slammed his brakes, and put the truck into reverse. As he gunned it backward, she sprinted after him, yelling for him to stop. But he fishtailed into the street. While he paused for a split second to shift into drive, she got a better look at him. Thirty-something, attractive, and oddly familiar.

Chapter 24

The Turbulent Present
Time had become meaningless

Sept. 9/10, middle of night (day 2/3 after the kidnapping)

Remi lay on a lumpy mattress in the basement of Yano's house, unable to sleep. The space was bigger than the storage room in the Portland B&B, but it was also dark and damp and full of cobwebs. Even with a hot-water heater nearby, she was still cold. She'd been down here since the afternoon with only two bathroom breaks. After the second one, she'd been given a sandwich, turkey this time, and a bottle of water. Earlier, she'd slept for several hours, but now it was the middle of the night, or so she assumed. Time had become meaningless.

Seth had left her hands free and she had access to a trouble-light on an extension cord. So now that the house was quiet, she explored all the nooks. Nothing but cobwebs and spiders. She moved carefully to a lumber-and-brick shelf and examined everything, but nothing seemed useful in terms of escape. The camping equipment, covered with a thick layer of dust, included a few tent stakes, but they weren't sharp enough to use for a weapon.

As if having a weapon would matter against three men. Since

Blake had found and confiscated the paring knife, he might be more inclined to search her pockets regularly. And they still had her dog. *Oh god,* she missed Tuck. He'd been her constant companion for all the time she could remember, and his absence felt like part of herself was missing. The last few weeks had left another hole in her heart too. Remi hated herself for it, but she also missed Thomas, or at least she missed what could have been.

No. He'd never had any real feelings for her. He'd lied from the beginning and betrayed her, probably for money. Who else knew to find her at the counselor's office? Remi touched her swollen nose and busted lower lip. Had Thomas known Yano would beat her? *The fucker.* She hated herself for being so gullible, for liking Thomas, for letting him penetrate her. Why had he hooked up with her? He could've just told Yano her location and habits and walked away. Why humiliate her too? Unless he also had a revenge grudge.

Fighting back tears and nausea, Remi paced the narrow room. She had to stop thinking about Thomas and focus on her predicament. She needed to stay physically strong and not let her left glute cramp up again. If she ever got a chance to run, she not only wanted to be able to, she needed to be fast. She was already dropping weight because her captors weren't feeding her enough to keep a runway model happy. She hoped Tuck was doing better. She'd pleaded with Yano to let doggo out of his cage for a while and he'd shrugged and said, "Maybe." Remi could only hope the crazy track-suit man would treat her boy decently.

The sound of a lock clicking made her freeze. At the top of the wooden stairs, the door opened and Blake snapped, "Let's go. We're heading out soon."

In the middle of the night? This couldn't be good. Remi trudged up the steps, relieved to exit the oppressive room despite her fear. Part of her was growing numb to her own fate. In the moment, she just wanted more food and water. Maybe a little lube for her dry lips. And a pain pill to stop her shakes. They weren't as bad as yesterday, but she didn't feel ready to go cold-turkey yet.

In the main house, she blinked at the bright lights. Blake led her down a hall to a small bathroom. "Yano wants you to shower and put on those." The big guy pointed to a stack of clothes on the back of the toilet. "Brush your teeth and put on makeup too. You need to look good for your next gig." He promptly stepped out. "You have ten minutes." Blake closed the door.

A shower! Remi quickly stripped off her clothes, wishing she could rinse her bra and panties before putting them back on, but wearing them wet didn't seem wise.

The warm water rushing over her skin felt glorious, and for a minute, she just stood there. Remembering her time limit, she used the generic shampoo to wash her hair, pits, and pubes, then reluctantly stepped out. After drying off and putting her own underclothes back on, she picked up the pink lacy camisole and pulled it over her head. It fit surprisingly well and showed plenty of cleavage. The white-denim shorts barely covered her butt and were too tight in the waist, so she left the zipper partway undone. What the hell did they have in mind for her?

The foundation they'd left out on the counter was too dark for her skin tone but she brushed it on anyway, then applied eye shadow and mascara. The overall effect wasn't bad, except for her wet hair. Not that she cared. Her only hope was to be passable at whatever new assignment they gave her. As long as she was useful, they would keep her and Tuck alive. Sooner or later, a chance to escape might present itself.

On impulse, she opened the medicine cabinet above the sink. Bandaids, aspirin, and a bottle of hydrogen peroxide. No help. Then she spotted something silver behind the box of bandages and reached for it. A pair of nail scissors. Sharp, but the blades were too short to do much more than break the skin. Useless, unless she stabbed someone in the eye. That could buy her a moment or two. But if Blake or Yano caught her with them, they would undoubtedly hurt her… again. Remi couldn't make up her mind.

Someone banged on the door, and she impulsively stuffed the little scissors into a front pocket in her shorts.

Seth pushed open the door. "You ready?"

"Except for the shakes. Can I have another Vicodin?"

He held out a pill. "Last one."

"Thanks." Remi filled the paper cup on the counter and swallowed the pill, downing all the water. Her skin was so dry it itched. She was grateful for Seth's occasional consideration. It made her think he had a heart in there somewhere. Not that he would ever let *her* escape, but he might spare doggo. "Hey, Seth. I appreciate your help with my withdrawals. You seem like a reasonable man."

He pulled back, surprised.

She had to try. "I know Yano may kill me. But poor Tuck doesn't deserve any of this. If I do end up dead, will you please let him go? Maybe drop him off at an animal shelter?"

"We'll see what Yano wants." Seth held out zip-ties.

Shit! The skin on her wrists already felt like road rash.

A few minutes later, she was back in Yano's man cave with the two thugs looming behind her. Yano was behind his desk, staring at a computer monitor, sipping from a tumbler that smelled like alcohol. After a moment, he stood, this time wearing jeans and a red polo shirt. Apparently, they all needed to look nice for this gig.

"We're driving west today, and I'll brief you on the way."

"Please tell me what's happening."

Yano smirked, but it wasn't a happy expression. "Remember when I said you put my wife in prison?" He stepped around the desk and leaned in close with bourbon breath. "Now you're gonna help me get her out."

Chapter 25

The Turbulent Present
You're just a distraction

Forty minutes later

Remi forced herself to unclench her grip on the steering wheel. Her shoulders ached from the tension of driving an unfamiliar car, on a winding forest road, in the dark... with a man in the passenger seat holding a gun. The Honda Civic was decades old and the interior was ragged, but it seemed to run well.

"Slow down," Yano commanded. "Our turn is coming up quickly."

Her foot off the gas, Remi squinted into the distance. All she could see were fir trees. From Yano's place, they'd headed west and driven by a few fields, passed what looked like a dam/fishing operation, then started climbing.

A few minutes later, she spotted a green-and-white state sign. Yano pointed. "Go left."

She rounded the turn, catching the lettering: *Stillman Creek Corrections.* Sickness filled her stomach and she suppressed the bile. Were Yano and his crew planning to barge in and shoot guards? She glanced in the rearview mirror. The van with Seth and Blake was still behind her.

"There's an abandoned lumber mill about a mile from here," Yano said. "That's our first stop."

Thank god. He had refused to answer her questions or tell her the plan until she "needed to know." Remi assumed the point of that was to keep her terrified. Or maybe to keep her from jumping out while she was behind the wheel.

Remi spotted a break in the tree-line and eased up, then turned into a dirt-and-gravel parking area. The old lumber mill loomed in the darkness beyond it.

"Drive alongside the building, then turn around and face the road."

The van pulled in behind her, and moments later, they all sat in the overhang, staring into the dark somewhere in southwest Washington.

"Can I get out for a moment? The burn on my butt really hurts from sitting too long." And not having enough medication in her system.

"No."

Prick. Remi leaned back and closed her eyes. She was learning not to think too much about what could or would happen next. She and Tuck were still separated, with him in the van, but they were both still alive. That was all that mattered.

After a short while, she sensed a change and opened her eyes. A glimmer of sunlight partly illuminated the scene.

Yano opened his door. "We got another twenty minutes or so before the work crew passes." He seemed to be talking mostly to himself as he climbed out. Moments later, she heard him peeing on the gravel.

When he got back in, he said, "We're gonna follow the bus. Not closely of course. I'm pretty sure it's goin' to Stillman State Park, but we're watching to be certain."

"How do you know?" Remi was so tense and bored, she wanted to keep him talking.

"Donna told me. I visit her regularly." Yano made a scoffing sound. "They denied my application at first, calling me a *known associate*." He made air-quotes around the term. "But I'm her husband and I don't have any charges or convictions related to her record. So I sued the state for the right to visit. And won." He laughed, but the harsh sound held no humor or joy. "It's the only reason I live in fuckin' Toledo."

Soon, on schedule, a white transport vehicle drove by, the rumble of its engine breaking through the quiet morning. The rig looked like a short bus with a truck front end. Maybe six or ten women were on board.

Remi reached for the ignition.

"Not yet."

Yano waited another minute, then gestured at her to go.

She rolled across the gravel and onto the asphalt. "We're not gonna run it off the road, are we? I don't want to hurt anyone."

"Me neither." Another nasty chuckle. "At least not today." A pause. "But I'll do what I have to."

When they reached the T intersection again, Yano directed her to turn left, toward the mountain. Remi didn't spot the white rig ahead, but it made sense that a work crew would head into the forest.

"More speed. We need to see them make the next turn."

They drove up the winding road for another twenty minutes,

with each curve a little more visible in the morning light, then caught sight of the white rig a few minutes before it veered left.

"Yep, the state park," Yano said. "That's good."

Remi couldn't take the suspense anymore. "Please explain my part in this. I don't feel ready." If nothing else, she needed a sweater or something if she had to get out of the car. The morning air was quite cool.

"Almost time." Yano reached over and rubbed the gun on her thigh. "You excited to be back in the game?"

She hated him for insinuating she might enjoy this shit show. "I want no part of it. I'm just trying to keep my dog alive."

"Then don't fuck up."

Her shoulders tensed again, and she rounded a corner too fast. The little car swung wide and Remi jerked the wheel to steer back onto the road.

"Hey!" Yano slammed the dashboard. "Watch out."

A scene flashed in Remi's mind. Another dark road trip with her driving. That snippet was all she remembered, except for the terror it left behind. "I'm sorry. But I'm nervous cuz you won't tell me anything."

"Pull over up here at the turnout and leave it running."

They had more daylight now, and Remi slowed when a massive gravel pile came into view. Next to it, metal brackets were stacked in long groups. The area was a state or county holding site for road-repair supplies. Remi drove behind the gravel, then Seth and Blake pulled in next to her.

"Stay here and don't move." Yano got out and the three men stood by the car chatting.

Remi rolled her window down a few inches but still couldn't

understand what they were saying. A moment later, Yano pivoted to her and gestured. "Pop the hood."

She searched around and finally found the lever. The car was probably thirty years old and beat to shit.

Yano fiddled with the engine for a moment, then came to stand by her window. She rolled it down the rest of the way, shivering in her skimpy clothes.

"Here's the deal." Yano lit a cigarette, the first she'd seen him smoke. "You're gonna drive by the transport van, then let your foot off the gas. The engine will sputter and die. Then you get out and walk back to the state park. A deputy will probably approach you immediately." A little chuckle. "They get nervous out here. But you explain that your car stalled and ask for their help. That's it. You're just a distraction."

Remi had a lot of questions.

Chapter 26

The Turbulent Present
Set up to be shot and killed

A few minutes later

With a gun to her head through the window, Yano reminded her what was at stake. "If you alert the deputy, we'll skin your little dog alive." He held out his phone. "Your mother will be next."

The screen showed an image of a woman coming out of a house. She was thin and dark-haired with a stern expression. Her again. The same conflicting emotions surfaced. Remi somehow loved and hated this woman without really knowing her.

Yano jerked the phone back. "Do your part and no one gets hurt today."

Remi nodded. It all seemed too easy. But she didn't know much about prison work crews or how they operated. Maybe they were slack. She assumed the inmates who went out in public, even deep in the forest, were nonviolent offenders from minimum security facilities. They probably had short sentences too, or at least not much time left, so the chance of them escaping was minimal. So why were Yano and his wife risking this?

He banged the roof of the car. "Let's go."

She rolled the Honda forward and pulled onto the road, then glanced over her shoulder. Yano climbed into the back of the van and it was soon behind her. After a few curves, she passed a junction with a numbered sign. In her rearview mirror, she watched the van veer onto the secondary road. They were headed to someplace behind the state park.

And she was alone in the car. This was her chance.

To do what? Yano had tampered with the engine, so she wouldn't get far. And if she didn't go through with her part, the plan would probably fail and Tuck would die. Guards might get killed too. The safest thing was to make this work.

As she passed the state park, Remi glanced over. Two female inmates in orange coveralls were painting a small building that looked like a bathroom. A male deputy in a brown uniform stood about twenty feet away, facing into the campground. He wasn't a big man, but that was definitely a holstered gun on his waist.

Oh fuck. What was she doing?

Remi let off the gas and the engine sputtered as expected. Soon the car stalled completely and she eased it off the road. After sucking in a deep breath, she climbed out. The morning chill made her shiver, and her nipples hardened under the thin camisole. Maybe that was the point of this stupid outfit. Or maybe she was just supposed to look ditzy and harmless.

She walked back toward the state park, heart pounding and trying not to limp. She didn't let herself hurry, even though she wanted to get it over with as quickly as possible. Yano had instructed her to be casual, but she'd accepted that she might end up in custody. The transport rig faced the road, parked between the open metal safety gates, effectively blocking out vehicles. Remi scooted alongside the rig and entered the campground.

As predicted, the deputy strode toward her, waving Remi off. "Move along!" he hollered. "This park is closed today."

Here goes. "My car broke down, and I don't have cell service out here. Can you radio for help?" Remi heard a breathless desperation in her voice.

"No. Just keep walking." The guard stared at her breasts.

"Seriously?" Remi shook her head. "I need to use the restroom first." She jogged toward the building being painted. The deputy charged over and grabbed her arm.

"Hey! Get off me!" Remi bellowed, hoping to attract the other guard's attention, wherever he or she was.

The deputy started pulling her toward the road. "You have to leave."

Remi resisted. "I just need to pee!"

The second officer didn't come running as expected. That was a problem. They needed both guards distracted so Blake, hiding in the nearby woods, could grab Donna and run to the van before either uniform realized an inmate was gone.

But the second deputy didn't materialize. *Shit!* And the one who had a grip on her seemed to be reaching for his gun. For a second, Remi wondered if she'd been duped, set up to be shot and killed by a corrections officer. Yano getting someone else to do his dirty work.

"Okay, I'm going." Remi shook her arm free and headed toward the road. The plan was for her to walk away, then cut through the woods to the second road and get picked up by Yano and the crew. But if Donna hadn't managed to escape, Yano would be enraged. He might beat her and Tuck to death. Remi glanced back once more to see if the second guard had left their post. Another inmate in orange coveralls now stood with the two painters, all three staring at Remi. But no second uniform. That meant Blake and Donna were still on hold.

The transport rig was right beside her, facing the road. What could she do that would get both guards attention? Grab something and break a window? That would get her cuffed and hauled away for sure, but it might not free Yano's wife or save Tuck.

Oh hell. Remi yanked open the bus-style door, trotted up the two steps, and scooted into the driver's seat. Behind her, she heard shouting.

"What the hell?"

"Get out of there!"

In the wide rearview mirror, she saw both deputies running in her direction, the second one, a woman, fifty feet behind. Remi's heart pounded in her ears. *Now what?*

The key was in the ignition.

Just do it! She started the engine, slammed the rig into gear, and pressed the accelerator. She shot past the gate posts and cranked the steering wheel to the left. The heavy rear end skidded on the gravel, but she managed to keep control. Remi gunned the engine and sped back in the direction they'd come from, heart pounding wildly.

One quick glance in the mirror was all she allowed herself. Both officers stood near the gate, feet spread and guns drawn. *Oh fuck!*

A shot rang out and she jerked forward. Two more shots quickly followed.

Fuckity fuck fuck!

Remi careened around a curve and kept going, watching for the trail between the two roads. Where the hell was it?

There!

She slammed the brakes, shut off the engine, and scurried out. She tossed the key into the culvert and bolted into the woods, leaving the rig in the middle of the road. Her burns screamed at her to stop, but she kept moving. The cut-through path was dark, narrow, and treacherous with tree roots. She tried to watch the ground and the direction she was running at the same time, but this wasn't a natural activity for her. She was sure she'd never hiked in the forest before, let alone ran. She glanced back to see if anyone was following and promptly tripped and fell.

When she stood, with her body and brain quiet for a moment, she heard an engine up ahead. The crew was nearby. Remi took off again, running and stumbling until she came to a small clearing where the van was parked. The sliding door opened and she climbed in. Yano, squatting in the back, slammed it shut, then Seth gunned the vehicle onto the road.

On her knees with her head down, Remi sucked in oxygen to slow her heart.

Yano pounded on her shoulder. "That was badass!"

From the front passenger seat, Blake glanced back. "I thought our chance was blown, then you stunned me with that move." He laughed. "Shocked those guards too."

"I tossed the key to stall them," Remi said through ragged breaths.

A full-throated laugh from Yano. "I might have to reward you for that."

"They never saw the van," Blake said. "So we're clear."

Remi finally sat back, cross-legged, and looked over at the escapee in orange coveralls, sitting in the captain's chair. Yano's wife was slender with long, silver-blonde hair pulled into a ponytail. She would have been pretty except for a narrow nose and cold eyes. "Hi, Riley."

Her heart skipped a beat. This woman scared her.

Donna scooted forward and slapped her face.

Oww!

The woman struck her again before Remi could catch her breath.

"One for each year in prison you cost me."

Tears welled in her eyes and Remi touched her cheek, still bruised from Yano's assault. Why hadn't she run when she had the chance? Tuck whimpered in his cage, reminding her of why not.

"I helped you with the stock thing and the prison escape. My debt is paid. Please let me go.

Yano let out a scoffing sound. "You're just getting started."

Oh fuck. She couldn't imagine what was next.

The van careened wildly to the left. *Oh yeah.* They were speeding along a mountainous road, and law enforcement across the state would soon be looking for them. Maybe they would crash. If they did, and she survived, she would grab Tuck and run.

Across from her, the reunited lovers were going at each other, mouths mashed together and hands in each others' pants. Were they gonna hook up right in front of her? Remi turned away and scooted toward doggo, whispering, "Hey Tuck. We'll be okay soon."

A few minutes later, the lovebirds backed off, panting.

"How much farther?" Yano asked.

Blake looked back. "Twenty minutes."

Remi calculated they were headed west, or maybe northwest, toward the coast.

When the van finally slowed, she peered out the windshield. Another small town. They took a few turns off the main road and pulled into a parking lot behind a tire store. Across the adjacent lot she spotted the backside of a rundown motel with brightly painted doors.

"Give us an hour or so in the room." Yano grabbed an overnight bag and scooted toward the sliding door. "But get in the other vehicle now."

The couple climbed out and headed toward the motel.

Stopping for sex seemed like a bad idea, but Remi hoped they would all get caught. It might be the only thing that could save her.

A few minutes later, Blake got out and opened the sliding door. "Let's go." He flashed his weapon just to remind her, then reached for Remi's arm. "The dog stays with Seth, so you'll have to behave yourself." He let out a laugh. "Not that anyone in hickville will give a shit if you holler."

As Remi stepped out, Blake laid his massive arm around her shoulders and squeezed. Gripping her tightly, the big guy led her across a strip of dried grass between the back parking lots. He unlocked a gray Toyota 4Runner, shoved her into the backseat, then got into the front on the passenger side.

A few minutes later, Seth opened the back hatch, dumped more duffle bags, then went back for Tuck's cage. Then they waited. Remi leaned back and closed her eyes again, grateful for a moment to rest. They'd gotten up around four that morning, and her stressed-out brain wanted to shut down. But she couldn't help but wonder about the prep of getting this backup vehicle into place. She'd been in the basement at Yano's for hours the afternoon before, so that must have given them time. The bigger question was what they had planned next. Remi whispered comforting words to Tuck, who was behind her in the crowded cargo space, then drifted off.

"Wow! Check her out." Blake's voice boomed in her ear. He was talking to Seth, but Remi sat up and looked out her window.

A heavyset woman with short dark hair had rounded the corner of the motel and was walking toward a small white car. Lettering on the side of the vehicle said *Fairview Realty*.

Seth stared. "She won't even get stopped lookin' like that."

That was Donna? In a wig and fat-suit? They had planned this well. "Where is she headed?"

"Mexico."

Blake punched Seth's shoulder. "She doesn't need to know that."

"Like it matters."

They didn't intend to let her live. Remi had known it was inevitable, but hadn't let herself believe it.

The door across from her opened and Yano climbed in, smiling like a man who'd just gotten a blow-job. "Now the fun begins."

Remi forced herself to breathe deeply. "What?"

"Remember my ring, Riley? The one you didn't like or deserve?" His tone held bitterness. "You're gonna steal it back, so I can give it to Donna, as I should have long ago."

Scattered memories crashed together in her head, giving her vertigo. Yes, her name was Riley, and she'd once worn a diamond Yano had paid for.

Chapter 27

The Old Life
Let's get this party started

Ocean Shores, WA, four and half years earlier (flashback)

A warm breeze, a moonlit walk on the beach, and the man she loved by her side. The moment was perfect and Riley had never been happier. She squeezed Luke's hand. "Thanks for planning this getaway. It's been wonderful."

"We needed it." Luke stopped, then scooted in front of her. "I love you, Riley. I want to spend the rest of my life with you."

Her pulse jumped. *Was he about to propose?* "I love you too." A lump in her throat.

Luke fumbled in his pocket, then dropped to one knee in the sand.

He was doing this. The waves crashing nearby were suddenly less soothing.

Luke opened a tiny jewel box and held it up. "Riley Brockwell, will you marry me?"

She smiled and the expression froze on her face. She loved Luke more than anything, but she wasn't ready for this. She wanted to get out of the Seattle area first, move someplace affordable where they could buy a house and have their own life. But she couldn't break his heart. She would go along, then stall on setting a date. "Yes, my love. I want to spend my life with you too."

"Perfect." He beamed with joy and jumped back up. "Let's get a ring on your finger."

Riley held out her hand.

"These were my mother's diamonds. My dad gave them to me when I told him I planned to propose." A catch in Luke's voice. "I had the engagement ring set with little sapphires because I know you like them."

She didn't want a dead woman's jewels, especially that wedding ring. The stone was embarrassingly huge and probably worth twenty or thirty grand. She would be too nervous to wear it casually, like some drug-store trinket.

Luke slid the smaller engagement cluster on her finger.

"It's lovely."

He drew her in for a hug, followed by an intense kiss. "I'm so glad you like it. I wanted to get you something special, but you know I can't afford it. Not yet."

Luke taught middle school and made about the same money she did as a cocktail waitress—but she worked half the hours. "It's fine. I know you're saving to buy a house."

"And have kids." He grinned. "The best things in life are insanely expensive."

"Yeah, right?" She wanted those things too, but she and Luke had only been together eight months. They needed more time to just be a couple.

"Come on." He grabbed her hand. "I have another surprise." He pulled her away from the ocean and toward the hotel.

Inside, Luke led her down a hall on the second floor. As they approached the end, the murmurs of a gathering grew into a roar.

Oh no. Riley wanted to turn and run. But Luke, beaming like he'd just won the lottery, opened the door and shouted, "Surprise engagement party!"

She swallowed hard. *What if she had said no?* Luke knew she wouldn't do that. She avoided confrontations and ended up being a go-along gal. Riley willed herself to step inside. The ballroom was haphazardly decorated with a rainbow of balloons and silver streamers, and the twenty-plus people were making enough noise for forty. None were related to her, and only a couple were friends. This was Luke's family, and his dad stood in the middle, voice booming, volume and confidence making him seem bigger than he actually was. Yano was always the center of attention and those around him were often laughing. Although their smiles could seem forced.

Trina, a co-worker, rushed toward Riley. "Congratulations, girlfriend! I'm so happy for you guys." She hugged Riley and kissed Luke's cheek.

Riley just kept smiling, her throat dry.

With Luke gripping her elbow, she walked through the cluster of cocktail tables, glad she was wearing a pretty summer dress. Toward the front, a DJ table and speakers filled a raised stage. At least she would have music and dancing to keep her occupied. She liked Luke's family, mostly, but they were overwhelming. As an only child raised by a widowed mother, she wasn't used to big loud gatherings. Her mom's family was back in Ohio, and her father had died before she had a chance to know him. Thinking about her mother was unsettling. They hadn't spoken since the night they'd met Yano and Luke at a charity fundraiser. Riley had been attracted to Luke on first sight, and her mom had taken an instant dislike to Yano. They'd had a horrible fight—with her mother bringing up previous boyfriends—and Riley had blocked her number, tired of the same old paranoid lectures.

"Hey, girl! Welcome to the family." Yano lurched at her, then crushed Riley in a powerful hug. "Another daughter." His pale face was flushed and his eyes cloudy. "You and Luke are meant for each other."

He wasn't as drunk as she'd seen him on football days, but the night was young. "Thanks."

Donna, the platinum ice queen, stepped toward her and pretended to kiss Riley's cheek. Instead she whispered, her breath bitter with vodka, "My girls will always come first."

Riley barely knew Luke's stepsisters and didn't know how she would displace them from whatever rank they held in the family hierarchy. As always, she ignored Donna's weird comments and pivoted toward Luke's brother, Matt, an older somewhat less-handsome version of her fiancé.

"Smiley Riley. About to become a Sebastiano. Welcome." Matt grabbed her shoulders.

She nodded and braced for another unwanted hug. She would never take their family surname. Her self-identification was one issue she was willing to fight for. Brockwell was her dad's name. He'd been killed in the line of duty and it was all she had left of him.

"Maybe not." Yano squeezed Matt's elbow. "Our business needs variation."

What was he talking about?

Donna nudged her husband. "No work stuff."

"Right. These kids need a drink." Yano squeezed Riley's arm. "What can I get you from the bar? My treat." He chuckled and gestured at the whole room. "All of this is on me."

"Just some orange juice," Riley mumbled. "You know I don't drink." After being a cocktail waitress for nearly a decade, she'd started to hate alcohol and what it did to people.

"Oh come on," Yano chided. "Don't be a party pooper. Have a damn drink."

Luke eased in front of her. "I'll get us both a glass of champagne to celebrate."

Donna gestured toward the DJ. "Let's get this party started!"

Luke headed for the service bar in the corner, while most of the crowd hit the dance floor. Yano soon had a contest going, with him being the judge, of course. While everyone was shaking their butts in a twerk-off, Trina grabbed Riley and walked her to the side of the room. "I brought this for you cuz I know how you are at these parties." Her friend pulled a tiny bottle of cannabis tincture out of her clutch purse and held out an eyedropper. "Open wide."

What the hell? Riley wanted to chill out for this Yano-loaded spectacle. She tipped her head back and Trina squeezed the bitter oil into the back of her throat.

"Thanks. And now I really do need something to drink."

Luke stepped up with a paper cup half full of orange juice, beaming. "At your service."

God, she loved him. Riley downed the juice. A moment later, the song changed and the three of them started grooving toward the dance floor. Yano called for a new competition, and one of his stepdaughters strutted into the center and got rolling with TikTok-style footwork. Her sisters cheered her on, then one of Luke's cousins strutted out there and tried to show her up. After two more contestants, Yano started chanting Riley's name and the cousins joined in. Luke gave her a friendly push. "You got this, girl."

Why not? The happy juice had started to smooth the edges already. Riley danced out to the middle and gave it her best shot. Working in bars, she'd seen plenty of fancy footwork and could imitate most of it. She was also light on her feet and loved to dance. The family clapped wildly for her, then JT, the youngest cousin, sashayed into the open space and outdid everyone.

Yano raised his nephew's arm in declaration of the win. JT reached for Riley to declare her a co-winner, but she eased away and bowed mockingly. "Thanks, but you rule." He was so sweet. After Luke, JT was her favorite in the Sebastiano clan. He wasn't as crazy and cocky as the others—except on the dance floor.

An hour later, Riley told Luke she was ready to go home. She was tired and, despite being a little stoned, couldn't handle any more shitfaced family members. Donna's youngest daughter had puked in her own purse, and Luke's uncle had taken off his shirt and was dancing wildly, shakin' his big belly with drunk pride.

"I put up with enough of this shit at work," she said, smiling to take the sting out.

"It's too early to leave," Luke argued. "My dad spent a lot of money on this party. Give him another hour, please."

No way. "Thirty minutes. And only if Uncle Ezra puts his shirt back on."

"Get real. I can't do miracles."

Riley laughed at the pained look on Luke's face. "I know. But the only way I can survive this is to keep dancing. And Ezra insists on doing that flab-jiggle thing right at me."

Luke laughed, and the sight and sound of his joy made her night.

"I'll get the bartender to cut him off. That's the best I can do. But we have to stay for a while." Luke kissed her, caressing her backside. Now she really wanted to leave. They had better things to do.

"Let's go dance," Luke coaxed. "I'll block your view of Ezra's shimmy."

Luke's smile was a magnet and she'd been helpless to resist him from the moment they'd met.

After a sexy slow song, Luke's brother and male cousins dragged him over to the service bar, yelling "Shots!" Riley stayed on the edge of the dance floor, letting the beat-heavy electronic music take over her mind and body, barely aware of the crowd.

"Hey, girl." Yano grabbed her elbow. He'd taken off his black jacket and unbuttoned the top of his burgundy-red shirt, but sweat still beaded on his receding hairline. "I have something for you guys. Come this way." He led her to a table in the corner away from the oversized speakers. "Wait here."

Riley watched him weave through the crowd, squeezing a few butts and shoulders on the way. He rounded up Luke from the bar, and the two men made their way across the room. Luke was taller, leaner, and better looking than his father, but they were obviously related, with the same nose and chin. As they reached the table, Yano sank into a chair. "I can feel my heart flopping around."

"You okay, Dad?" Luke sat next to him.

"I'm fine." Yano gestured for Riley to sit too. "I'm more than fine. I'm so happy about your engagement, I've decided to give you guys a sizable down payment for a house."

AfterStrike

Wow. Their own home. They could finally get out of their noisy apartment complex and live someplace with a backyard for Tuck. Riley wanted to happy dance, but she waited for Luke to respond.

"Sweet!" Luke gave Yano a one-armed hug. "That changes everything for us. We would've had to save up for years."

"I know." Yano planted a sloppy kiss on Riley's face. "I want to see your beautiful babies before I die of a heart attack."

Riley smiled. Yano could be loving and generous as well as fun. But tomorrow, he might not remember making the offer. Still, if he did follow through, she would reconsider staying in the Sea-Tac area. She knew it would be good for Luke to get away from his family for a while and be his own person, but on the two occasions she'd brought it up, he'd looked at her like she'd suggested moving to the moon. At least Luke had a job that wasn't connected to his dad's car dealership or Donna's real estate business—unlike most of the other family members. And they all helped Yano with *special projects*, whatever they were.

Which reminded Riley to ask Luke later about the terms of the down payment. Sometimes expensive gifts came with obligations, and she didn't want any surprises down the road.

Chapter 28

The Old Life
Look how that turned out

Tacoma, three years and three months earlier (flashback)

Riley climbed out of Luke's old Jeep and stared at the massive house. She'd been here many times, but Yano's wealth and flamboyancy still overwhelmed her. In addition to the mini-tower that jutted up from the roof in back, the entrance sported a long portico with an extended roof that guests could park under and not get wet on their walk to the door. In the dark, rainy moment, she appreciated the feature. But this visit made her nervous. Yano had summoned them for a "family chat." Not a dinner invitation or a fun backyard barbecue with the gang. A private meeting with just the two of them.

As they walked up, Riley reached for Luke's hand. "Are you sure Yano's not mad because I missed Lexi's baby shower?" His oldest stepdaughter was having her third child, and Riley hadn't taken a night off work to attend.

"I'm sure." Luke gave her hand a gentle squeeze. "Donna might be though."

"Yeah. I figured."

The ice queen greeted them at the door and led them back

146

to Yano's study. On the way, she elbowed Riley. "Don't look so nervous. You know how Yano is. He just likes to chat in person about important stuff." Donna pushed open the double doors, and they walked in. Big screen TVs and high school sports trophies lined the walls.

Behind the oak desk, Yano sipped a tumbler filled with bourbon. "Hey, you lovebirds. Thanks for stopping by."

"Of course." Luke sat in a leather armchair and gestured for Riley to do the same. "What's up, Dad?"

"I'll get right to the point. When are you guys gonna give me a grandchild?"

That was it? Relieved, Riley almost laughed. In the last year, they'd eloped and bought a house, but apparently that wasn't enough.

Luke squirmed. "We want to wait."

"For what?" Yano glanced back and forth, his black eyes intense.

She'd prepared for this. "Until we have enough saved so I can take a year off to bond with our baby." She also wanted to buy a few acres someday and operate a breeding and boarding business for dogs, her lifelong dream. But she'd never mentioned that to Yano. Donna hated dogs, and Riley had to leave Tuck at home when they visited.

"Just throw away your birth control pills." Yano gulped some bourbon. "You're pushin' thirty. All this planning and saving is working against you."

Pushin' thirty? That hurt. Riley still felt young, and she worked hard to stay skinny and attractive.

"Come on, Dad. This is our decision." Luke meant well, but he sounded weak.

Yano swirled his drink, silent for a moment. "I'm still pissed off that you eloped instead of letting me host a proper wedding." Yano set his drink down, then stood and nodded at Riley. "Would you excuse us for a moment? Go join Donna in the theater."

Riley bit back a smart-ass retort, then strode out. Halfway down the hall, she stopped and turned back. Yano had no right to dismiss her that way. She and Luke were partners, no secrets. As she neared the den, she had second thoughts and paused. No point in causing Luke more problems. He was already having a hard time with everything.

She'd left the door ajar when she walked out, and now she heard Yano raise his voice. Riley stepped closer to listen.

"This isn't optional," Yano snapped. "I shelled out thirty grand for a down payment so you wouldn't have to pay mortgage insurance. You owe me."

"I thought it was a gift." Luke's voice was subdued.

"Are you new here?" Yano scoffed. "You know better."

"I'll get a weekend job and pay back the money," Luke countered. "As I've told you, I want a different kind of life. That's why I borrowed thousands to get a teaching degree."

"Look how that turned out." Yano shook his head. "You hate your job."

"No. I just hate what it's become." Luke sounded resigned. "But I really don't want to be part of your scams."

What the hell? Riley inched closer.

"Don't act like you're better than me." Bitterness in Yano's tone. "My *projects* paid for all your extras. Summer basketball camps, winter ski trips, yearly island vacations. You don't get to enjoy the fruits of my labor while condemning the source. You're already part of this."

A long silence.

"You want the good life?" Yano prodded. "Nice things for your kids? I'm not asking you to join my business with Scott, just to file another claim."

Riley wanted to burst in and stand behind Luke, to declare they could achieve all that on their own without scamming anyone. Even more, she wanted her husband to stand on his own and tell his father to *suck it*.

But Luke didn't. "Okay. I'll do it."

"Great. Come into the dealership and pick up a nice car. The payouts are much higher on luxury models."

"I know." Luke sounded defeated. "So are the insurance payments."

"So?" Yano scoffed. "It's only for a couple months and you'll earn it back ten times over."

Riley didn't want to hear any more. She hurried back up the hall.

On the drive home, she put in her earbuds and listened to music, still too upset to reason with Luke. Once they were in the house, she went to the kitchen and made a cup of mint tea.

Luke followed her. "What's wrong?"

"I overheard the conversation with your dad."

His eyes clouded with shame. "What part?"

"Seriously?"

Luke grabbed a beer from the fridge, then looked at her with his please-don't-hate-me expression. "I don't have a choice. We took the money for the down payment on the house."

She stared at him, unblinking. "You said it was a gift, that we didn't have to pay it back."

"I said we didn't have to make cash payments, but that we might owe him a favor or two." He gulped his beer.

Riley had hoped to cool off, but her anger was still building. "A favor is house-sitting or mowing someone's lawn. He wants you to help him commit a crime."

"It's just insurance fraud. And those companies are so big and so loaded with cash, it's a drop in the bucket to them." Now Luke wouldn't look at her. "You're the one always saying insurance is a license to steal. So we'll be taking some of it back."

"It's still wrong." She didn't know the details of what he was expected to do and didn't want to.

"It could get me out of teaching." Luke eased toward her and tried to hold her hands.

Riley pulled away. She couldn't allow him to touch her or she would give in. "I know you hate the job now, and I'm sorry. But you have to stick it out until we find another way."

"You have no idea what it's like to stand in front of a class where no one is paying attention." Luke chugged half his beer and paced the kitchen. "They're looking at their phones, throwing things, wrestling. These kids have no fear, because there are no consequences. Not at school or at home. I can't do it anymore."

"Then find something else."

"That pays thirty-five bucks an hour?" He rolled his eyes. "I'd have to go to trade school, and we don't have time for that. We have a mortgage." He gestured around their modest house.

Riley racked her brain for ideas. "You could become a tutor. Or get an online teaching job."

Luke stopped in front of her. "Did you hear Yano mention the hundred-thousand-dollar payout?"

How had she missed that? "Are you serious?"

"As a heart attack. Except, I have to fake an accident instead." Luke seemed resigned. "Of course, Yano gets a third for orchestrating everything and making sure the paperwork is filed correctly."

A series of images and events came together for Riley in a clarifying moment. "That's why your cousins and stepsisters are always bruised or wearing an arm-sling or whatever. They're all part of the scams."

Luke lifted his shoulders in a small shrug. "Nobody gets seriously hurt. And they all have more money and free time than we do." His voice excited now, he started to pace again. "I could quit teaching and you could start breeding terriers and dachshunds. Or have a baby. Or both. One or two of these gigs will change our lives."

She wanted all that more than anything. But at what price?

Chapter 29

The Turbulent Present
The jackass had a gun in his hand

Sept. 10, Wilsonville (day 3 after the kidnapping)

D allas went out for a quick early morning run, then made scrambled eggs with the stuff in the fridge. Might as well not let food go to waste. She'd grown up poor, saddled with drug-addicted parents, so she'd learned from an early age to take care of herself, adapt to whatever came at her, and never waste anything. As she ate, she called her boss to update him. He surprised her by picking up. She'd hoped to leave a message and not get into the sticky details of how she was handling the situation.

"Dallas, what have you got?"

"I'm ninety percent sure Remi Bartel is our witness, Riley Brockwell. "I'm staying in her place and"—Dallas glanced around—"she lives like someone on the run. Few possessions, few acquaintances, and pays cash for everything."

"Did you find her phone or any documentation?"

"No."

She heard him sip coffee, then ask, "Was she kidnapped or did she just run again?"

"If she ran, she left twenty grand in her safe, so it seems unlikely."

"You opened her safe?" It was more of a statement—with a hint of concern.

Dallas regretted sharing that detail. "Her roommate said I could."

"You know it's better if you don't tell me these things."

"I know. Sorry." Better not mention that she hadn't contacted the local police yet either.

"What else?"

"Her vehicle was still in the parking lot hours after her counseling appointment, then it disappeared overnight." She paused to swallow another bite of eggs. "Either the thugs came back and dumped it in the river, or it was towed. I'm heading out to the tow yard right after this."

"I assume you've searched her place. Find anything useful? Maybe some evidence against Sebastiano?" Radner sounded amused by his own wishful thinking.

Finished with her meal, Dallas got to her feet. "No. But I think I found a safe deposit key. No idea where the box is located though."

"Then you'd better find our witness."

"I'm on it." She ended the call.

Tidewater Towing was just outside of town, a fenced area with an old mobile home for an office, surrounded by an impound lot with a dozen vehicles. Next door, a Pick N Pull car-parts business spread over several acres with hundreds of wrecked or abandoned vehicles. The same guy probably owned both. Dallas spotted a dark-green Mazda just inside the open gate. She drove past it and parked in front of the trailer, which sported a swastika, sloppily spray-painted under the business name and logo. As she got out, she touched the Glock under her blazer, giving her a measure of comfort.

Dallas climbed the weathered wood steps to the dented metal door and pushed it open. The dark space reeked of cigarettes and engine oil but otherwise looked clean on the surface. She smiled at the barrel-shaped old man behind the cluttered desk. "I'm Agent Dallas with the FBI."

After a moment of startled silence, he said, "Joe Tidewater. What can I do for you?"

"I need to see the Mazda you picked up two nights ago. It was in the lot behind Craig's Computers."

"You got any paperwork?"

She showed him her badge. "The owner was kidnapped, and I'm trying to find her."

He scowled. "Why haven't I heard anything from the police?"

Because they're incompetent? "They don't have the same information the bureau does. We know Remi Bartel is in danger."

"I can't let you into the car without a title or registration."

"If this is about money, I'll pay the impound charges." She pulled a cash clip from her pocket. "Two hundred?"

"It's about ownership… plus the fees."

Dallas remembered the spare key in her blazer pocket. "I'll be right back with the title." She smiled sweetly and walked out.

She jogged straight to the Mazda and unlocked it. The old guy was probably watching her, but what could he do? Call the police? She was supposed to chat with them anyway. She yanked open the driver's door and did a quick visual search. Nothing.

Not even a gum wrapper. Leaning in, she opened the console between the seats. A cellphone! She grabbed it, slipped it into her shoulder bag, then hurried around to the passenger side. The glovebox held only registration papers and a stack of fast-food napkins.

"Hey! Get out of there!" The old guy was barreling toward her.

"I have the key, so we'll call that ownership." Dallas scanned the backseat. Nothing but a couple of chew toys.

"Get away from the car or I'm calling the police!"

Dallas stepped back and pivoted toward him. The jackass had a gun in his hand. Pointed at the ground, but still...

Time to go. Still, she didn't want to get shot on her way out. "I'm working with the Wilsonville police and they know I'm here." She gave him a scathing look. "I'm trying to find a woman who's been kidnapped." Dallas eased toward her Kia rental, not willing to turn her back on him. "By the way, threatening a federal officer is a felony, so you should put that weapon away."

Tidewater blinked, but didn't back down.

Dallas kept sidestepping until she reached her car door. "Have a nice day.'"

Half expecting him to shoot at her tires, she glanced in her rearview mirror as she drove through the gate. The old guy hadn't moved. *Good.* She didn't want to deal with the local cops right now, or maybe at all. If they hadn't located the missing woman's car, they obviously weren't searching for her and would just slow her down with pointless questions.

On the drive back, Dallas passed a big metal building that said, *Bartel's Meat Packing.* Did Remi/Riley have family here or had she randomly chosen the name as her new ID? People on the run didn't go see their families… unless they were stupid. That was the best way to get tripped up. It seemed certain their witness had chosen a new name and was, in fact, Riley Brockwell.

Back at the cottage, Dallas searched Brockwell's phone, which took all of five minutes. The woman had no saved text messages and only five contacts, three of whom Dallas had met. The fourth was the daycare where she'd worked, and the fifth, Thomas, might be the new boyfriend. But without a last name, he might be hard to track. Dallas called his number and left a message. "Hey, Thomas. This is Agent Dallas with the FBI. I'm looking for Remi Bartel. If you have any information about her, please call me." She left her number, just in case she was dealing with a landline.

If Thomas was a good guy, he would return the call. If not, he was probably a suspect. The man in the truck from the night before came to mind. She hadn't been able to place him, but if he'd turned up in Brockwell's life after the news story featuring Tuck, he might be part of Yano's crew.

Frustrated, Dallas paced the house, trying to decide her next move. She wanted to be out there, searching, but where? She considered heading north to the Seattle-Tacoma area, where Yano had operated his fraud scams, but it seemed unlikely they would take Brockwell there. If the plan was to eliminate her, they'd likely dumped her body somewhere local. Why else would Yano come after her? Unless he had some sick revenge fantasy to act out. But even if Brockwell was dead, they still needed to find the perps. If Yano's crew had transported her body, technicians would likely find her DNA in the vehicle, a solid piece of evidence for a conviction. So she had to find the transport vehicle—if it wasn't the Mazda.

Dallas called the Portland field office and was finally connected to the contact person Radner had set up.

"Hey, Dallas. Sorry I haven't been in touch. But I figured you'd call me if you needed anything." Agent Sarkey sounded young and male.

"I found the missing woman's car. It's at Tidewater Towing in Wilsonville. Can you get technicians down here to process it?"

"Sure thing."

"The owner carries a gun and doesn't like feds, so send armed backup with the technicians. Maybe get the local cops involved too."

"Damn. I'll head down there myself." A pause. "You'll be there?"

"No. I'm heading north to Yano's old stomping ground. Will you line up a contact for me in the Seattle bureau?"

"Of course."

"Thanks."

Dallas loaded her luggage into the Kia, preparing to leave, then sat back down at Brockwell's laptop for one more search. There had to be something useful. She gave up after twenty minutes. The witness had kept mostly offline and didn't save any files or receipts. Her thoughts came back to Thomas, who might be key to all of this. Dallas took out Brockwell's phone and texted him: *Hey, call me. I need help.*

Maybe that would get his attention. She wished she'd done that before identifying herself as a federal agent. Dallas booted up her own laptop, wrote a short report about her morning discoveries, then opened her email and attached the file to her boss. As she pressed Send, a Google alert landed. For *Donna Mackey*.

A shiver shot up her spine. She clicked the link, which took her to the Washington State Police website. The breaking news report was brief: *Inmate Donna Mackey escaped from a Stillman Creek Corrections' work crew early this morning with the help of an unknown woman and probably others.*

Dallas sucked in a sharp breath. Mackey was Yano's wife, and Riley Brockwell's testimony had put her away. This case was suddenly a lot more pressing.

Chapter 30

The Turbulent Present
Short timers with no motive to escape

Minutes later

After sending her boss another update, this one regarding Mackey's escape, Dallas checked Google Maps, then hurried to her vehicle. The Stillman Creek Prison was two and a half hours away, two heading north on the freeway, then another thirty minutes west into a forested area in southern Washington. She chuckled at her reference to *forested area*. The whole damn Pacific Northwest was covered with giant Christmas trees. Amazing, overwhelming, and so different from Arizona.

On her way to the freeway ramp, she passed Bartel's Meat Packing again and wondered if the place had any significance for Riley Brockwell. Probably not. Dallas had watched Brockwell's interrogation/confession before leaving the taskforce and hadn't been impressed. The woman seemed sincere but not particularly bright. Yet Brockwell's commitment to a careful, out-of-sight lifestyle made Dallas reconsider her assessment. Unfortunately, the witness hadn't traveled far enough away from Tacoma or put any distance between herself and the interstate. Had Brockwell's car broken down?

Dallas took the on-ramp to the freeway and glanced in her rearview mirror for one last look at Wilsonville.

Was that the black pickup she'd seen in Brockwell's driveway?

Probably not. Hundreds of such testosterone-mobiles were on the roads, especially in rural areas. But she would keep an eye on it anyway.

Hours later, she drove up a winding road through a wooded hillside, occasionally glancing in her rearview mirror. She hadn't seen the black truck since she left the freeway. When she spotted the artsy state sign, Dallas turned onto an even steeper drive that was mercifully short. The prison, a cluster of fifties-built, single-story buildings, sat at the top of a butte. If you had to serve time, this was the place to be, a minimum-security facility with few inmates and a stunning view. Especially if you were privileged enough to join a work crew that left the property every day.

As Dallas exited her Kia, a male deputy waddled toward her in heavy boots. "Get back in your vehicle. No visitors today."

"Agent Dallas, FBI. I'm here about Donna Mackey." She held out her badge. "I just have a few questions."

He touched his goofy brown hat. "We've got this handled, ma'am."

"I'm sure you do. But the bureau is looking for a missing woman and *we need your help*." *Appeal to his ego.*

"We'll see with the warden." He clumped toward the front building, a windowless bunker with slate-blue vinyl siding. Dallas followed.

Inside, they passed through a low-tech, security foyer and walked down a short hall to a small office. At the sight of her, the man behind the desk pushed to his feet. Tall, dark, fifty-something, and likely Native American. Chiseled features made him a human work of art. Dallas held out her hand and introduced herself.

"Warden Dan Birdsong. Have a seat."

She would have preferred to stand, but wanted to keep him at ease. As she sat, she sensed the deputy hovering in the doorway.

"What can I do for you?" Birdsong's voice was deep and hypnotic, like the Chief character in the old movie, *One Flew Over the Cuckoo's Nest*.

"I'd like details about Donna Mackey's incarceration and escape."

The deputy stepped forward. "You said you were looking for a missing woman."

"I am. Her name is Remi Bartel, aka, Riley Brockwell. She might be the person who assisted in Mackey's escape."

Birdsong furrowed his dark eyebrows. "What's the connection?"

"Donna Mackey's husband, Aden Sebastiano."

"We're familiar with him." A hint of contempt.

"He visited his wife?" Dallas was surprised the prison allowed it.

"He sued and won the right." The warden's shoulders stiffened. "How is he connected to the missing woman?"

"Brockwell was his daughter-in-law, and she testified against Donna and another family member, then disappeared right before Yano's trial started." Dallas shifted in the hard metal chair. Old funky prisons had limited budgets. "At the time, we thought Yano might have killed, threatened, or bribed her. Then about three days ago, a woman disappeared from Wilsonville, Oregon, and we have reason to believe she's our witness."

"You think Yano found her?"

Dallas nodded. "This morning, his wife escaped from one of your work crews. The report says she had assistance from another woman. What did the accomplice look like?"

Birdsong reached for a file. "Thirty-something, light-brown hair, and scantily dressed."

That could be Brockwell… or a million other women. But at least the description didn't rule her out. "Any images?"

"No. The crew was working at a state park, and our deputies don't wear cameras."

Dallas wanted to believe Brockwell was still alive. But once Yano had used her to help his wife go free, what would happen to Brockwell now? Was she still of any value? Maybe not to him, but his thugs might keep her around as a sex slave. A horrifying thought. Another dark possibility: Maybe Brockwell had rejoined the family business.

"Anything else you need to know?" Birdsong's deep voice was strangely soothing.

"How long has Donna Mackey been here and how much time did she have left?"

The warden scanned the file on his desk. "Transferred here nine months ago after she completed a cognitive behavior program and still had twenty-six months on her sentence."

Two years. Why risk escape with so little time left? Dallas recalculated. For a prisoner, two years could be an eternity. "Do you have an address on file for Aden Sebastiano?"

"The state police have already been there. It's a vacant lot." He sounded ready to wrap things up.

Dallas had more she wanted to know. "How predictable were the work crews? Do they go out to the same area for extended periods? Or do they mix it up just to prevent this kind of thing?"

"They stay in the same area until they've completed the work." He leaned toward her, seeming tense for the first time. "But we have to be flexible to accommodate our staff, the state's priorities, and a variety of other elements, including the weather. But the crew members are short-timers with little motive to escape."

"That part puzzles me too." Dallas wanted to know what the couple was thinking. "Do you have any letters or emails Yano and Mackey sent each other? If so, I'd like to see them."

"We read every correspondence at the time it takes place. They didn't plan this on our watch."

Dallas smiled to reassure him. She hadn't meant to assign blame. "I'd still like to get copies to take with me."

Birdsong picked up a secondary folder and handed it to the deputy behind her. "Make a copy of these for our federal guest please."

The short man grunted and scurried down the hall.

Dallas stood. "Can I see Mackey's cell?"

"The women sleep in dorms, and we've already checked her bed and belongings." His tone suggested her time was up.

"Thanks for your help."

Birdsong stood too. "Do you have any idea where our prisoner is?"

"No. But if it were me, I'd be on a plane or a boat, headed out of the country." A frustrating thought. If Yano was fleeing the country, the less baggage the better. And Brockwell was likely just baggage at this point.

"I wouldn't be sure about that." The warden lowered his voice.

"You know how it goes. Mackey's a fifty-year-old woman and a nonviolent offender, so her risk to the community is minimal. After a few days, we'll all get back to business as usual. There won't be a statewide manhunt."

"I understand. Priorities, budgets, and all that." A little disappointing.

"I'll walk you out." Birdsong gestured toward the door.

Dallas took her time moving down the hall and back through the security area, hoping to get the copies before she left.

The deputy met them at the door and handed her a file.

"Thanks. I'll keep you posted if I uncover anything."

Chapter 31

The Turbulent Present
Every once in a while just to fuck with me

Sept. 10, Tacoma (day 3 after the kidnapping)

A ferry horn sounded, waking Riley from a fitful sleep. Despite the setting sun and disorientation from nodding off in one place and waking up in another, she knew they were in the Seattle-Tacoma area. Her hometown. She'd been born in Ohio, but this was where she'd spent most of her life, traveling around the waterways and inhaling the ocean air. Memories of her childhood flashed in her mind like a digital carousel ad. Crashing her bike on a downhill when she was six. A middle-school assembly when she'd learned a classmate had died. Making out with her high school boyfriend, Jason, under the bleachers at a basketball game. So many memories were coming back now, but her last year or so in this area was still a void, a time and place she never wanted to revisit.

They took the Port of Tacoma exit and drove east past gas stations, big retailers, and hotels with casinos. After a while, it was too dark to see much, but they weaved their way across the city until they were deep in a suburb she didn't know. When they turned onto a cul-de-sac, Riley's pulse escalated. After helping a prisoner escape, stealing a ring shouldn't have scared her, but it did. She sensed the stakes were escalating, that Yano would take bigger risks now that he'd secured his wife's freedom. The diamond was valuable, for sure, but Yano's need to steal it back had to be personal and petty. But she'd given up trying to understand him long ago. Narcissistic thought processes were too convoluted to follow. Yet she was curious to know who had the ring and why. She hadn't let herself think about it until now, sleeping for most of the trip north to mentally escape her circumstances. But to pull this off, she needed information.

"Who has the ring? What can I expect to encounter?" Terrifying thoughts popped into her head. Guard dogs, screaming alarms, a man with a gun.

"Copeland. You remember him?"

The name sounded familiar. For a brief second, she pictured an older man in a gray suit, sitting across a table from her. "Is he a detective?"

"Bingo."

"How did he get the ring?"

Yano tipped his head, staring at her with an odd mix of skepticism and anger. "You had the diamond, and now he has it. So either you gave it to him or he took it from you."

None of that made sense. Why had she been involved with a detective? "How do you know Copeland still has it? Why not sell the diamond?"

Yano's eyes clouded. "He sends a picture every once in a while just to fuck with me."

That sounded messed up. But Yano had somehow remained free while his wife had gone to prison. Riley now realized those circumstances were mostly her doing. Apparently, the detective wasn't happy about Yano's escape from justice.

"I'm sure Copeland keeps the ring somewhere close by," Yano said, bitterness dripping from his words. "Maybe in his desk or nightstand, so he can savor his possession of it."

They turned onto another street, and Yano tapped Seth's shoulder. "Pull over and park behind that RV. We'll be out of sight from the house."

Riley's heart started to pound. Stealing from a cop seemed like a suicide mission. Especially at this hour. Night had fallen and the street was quiet, families settled in for the evening. "How do you know he's not home?"

"We did the recon," Blake said from the front passenger seat. "Copeland plays late afternoon golf with a friend, then they stop for pizza and beer at Joey's. We've got at least an hour."

Yano handed Riley a dark-gray hoodie and a pair of black sweatpants. "Put these on over your clothes."

Now that the sun was down, she was glad for the extra layer. Lifting off the seat to get the sweatpants on triggered a moment of intense glute pain, but it didn't last. *Thank god.* She hadn't taken any medication since early that morning. Or had it been yesterday? Time no longer meant anything and she'd learned to zone out for hours.

After she pulled on the hoodie, Yano handed her a mini can of spray paint and a cordless drill. "Keep these in your pouch and move quickly."

He'd coached her on the steps once already, and now she just wanted to get it done. Maybe this would be her last debt payment. What followed might be a bullet to her head—after digging her own grave in the forest—but at least this wide-awake nightmare would be over. She reached into the cargo area and stuck her fingers into Tuck's cage. He licked her and whimpered. "You'll be okay." It was all she could muster and probably a lie, but she had to give poor doggo whatever comfort she could. Her only hope was that Seth, who seemed to have some compassion, would let him go when this was over.

Riley grabbed the plastic bag from the floor. After their last fast-food meal, Yano had stuffed it with styrofoam containers to make it look like a food delivery. If anyone asked, she worked for Door Dash.

Yano leaned over and kissed her cheek. "Bring me the ring, and I'll let you live."

She tried not to recoil—just in case he meant it. But she didn't believe him.

"Fuck it up, and I'll kill your dog and your mother."

That she believed. But her mom wouldn't go down easily.

Out of the car, Riley hustled along the sidewalk. Despite her insane circumstances, she felt lighter and more agile than she had in months, thanks to their starvation diet and her burns starting to heal. Or maybe it was just adrenaline pumping in her veins.

Copeland's place was a modest single-level in a neighborhood full of newer two-story houses. Or at least they looked new in what little light she had from their outdoor lamps. Riley hurried up the empty driveway and turned onto the stone path. As she reached the front steps, a porch light came on, startling her. She stumbled but caught herself and stared at the entry. The door didn't open and no one called out. The light fixture was motion sensitive.

Keeping her head down, she rang the doorbell as instructed and nothing happened. No dogs barked and no footsteps hurried toward her. Riley quickly pulled the rattle can, stood on her tiptoes, and spayed the camera lens in the corner of the covered entry. What was the point? The camera had already captured her hooded image. Hands shaking, she extracted the drill. This part made her nervous. Drills were noisy and dangerous.

Just do it!

The doorknob's fancy lever threw her off for a moment, but it had a key slot like any other. She pushed the wide drill bit against the narrow slot, braced herself, then pressed the tool's trigger. The drill bucked and growled, but she leaned her weight into it and resisted the urge to look around. The noise seemed raucous in the quiet neighborhood, but it wouldn't last long and her body was blocking much of it from traveling.

Once she ground through the metal cap, the bit plunged quickly into the hollowed-out area, and she heard it chew up the locking mechanism. Riley shoved the heavy drill back into her pouch, then yanked on the handle. The door pushed open a few inches. Success.

"Anyone home? I have your order," she called out as she stepped inside.

No response. Riley set the plastic bag on a narrow foyer console and hurried down the hall. The first door was closed, and she opened it slowly. Cops could be paranoid and devious. The room was a pretty guest space with a pink blanket and a stuffed panda on the bed. For a visiting granddaughter? She moved to the second door on the other side, which stood open. More promising. Riley stepped in.

Near the window was a small desk with an old, tower-style computer on the floor next to it. *People still used those?* Weight-lifting stations filled the rest of the room, and an open closet revealed a floor-to-ceiling collection of CDs. Those were obsolete too. Curious, she stepped over to the closet and pulled a disk from the top of a stack. *Cheerleader-spank porn.* Not her thing, but whatever. Still, there were hundreds of disks. Were they all porn? He must have started collecting before the internet.

She shoved the CD back, hurried to the desk, and quickly searched the drawers. A hodgepodge of office supplies filled most of the space, except for a bag of fun-sized Butterfingers. The larger bottom drawers held files in cream-colored folders. Gut instinct, plus Yano's remarks about Copeland "taunting" and "savoring" made her think the ring wasn't in the paperwork anywhere.

She ducked into a bathroom, took the opportunity to pee, then checked the medicine cabinet. Lots of shaving and footcare stuff, but no jewelry or meds. Until that moment, she hadn't realized she was hoping to find pain pills or tranquilizers. But who wouldn't crave them under this kind of stress?

At the end of the hall, she found the master bedroom. Riley went straight to the tall dresser and yanked open the top drawer. Socks. *Thank goodness.* She'd sort of expected to find a collection of sex toys. Rummaging under the pile, she found a battered box of condoms. The next three drawers held only t-shirts and jeans.

Scanning the room, she spotted a book on the nightstand by the bed. And reading glasses. And Butterfinger wrappers. His personal space. Riley hurried over. Next to the alarm clock sat a hinged, wooden jewelry case the size of a tissue box. She opened the lid and there sat the marquise-shaped diamond. Memories flooded her, some joyful, some furious, but she pushed them aside and grabbed the ring. The most secure place to transport it was her finger, but she couldn't bear to put it on. She shoved it deep into a pocket in her sweatpants and turned to leave.

The rumble of a garage door opening made her heart thump. *Shit!* Copeland was home early. Riley sprinted up the hall, hoping to dash out the front door before he came in from the garage. He might not even see her. She rounded the archway into the living room.

And almost ran into Blake.

What the hell? Was he checking on her?

The big guy pressed a hand to her mouth, his face contorted in determination. In his other hand he held his gun. This one seemed different, bigger than the one he'd threatened her with.

Footsteps sounded in the kitchen.

Riley wanted to run, but where? If she crossed the living room to the front entrance now, Copeland would see her. And maybe shoot her. Retired cops carried weapons too. Where was the back door?

A familiar gray-haired man stepped into the dining area.

Before she could move, Blake raised his gun and fired. The blast, although muffled, filled the room.

Paralyzed with fear, she watched the detective pull a weapon from his jacket and shoot back, a deafening sound.

A second muffled shot rang out almost simultaneously. The detective stumbled forward, then dropped to his knees, blood gushing from his neck.

No! Not this guy! For a moment, Riley was torn, her instinct to rush over and help him. But she knew it was pointless, and the horror of his death was too much to bear. Riley bolted for the front door and out into the night. As she pounded down the driveway, Blake caught up to her and grabbed her hair, then kept running, dragging her along. He turned toward the RV and Riley stayed with him, pain and fear driving her.

In the 4Runner, she burst into sobs.

"You get the ring?" Yano held out his hand.

Still crying, Riley dug the diamond out of her pocket and handed it over, while Seth backed up.

"Go easy," Yano yelled at the driver. "Nothing suspicious!"

He pivoted to Blake. "What the hell? Did Copeland get off a shot? The whole freakin' neighborhood probably heard it."

"It grazed me!" The big guy bellowed. "I need some kind of bandage."

"Ah shit." Yano grumbled, then leaned into the back to rummage around in a duffle bag. He handed Blake a sock. "Use this to soak up blood, while I find something to hold it in place."

As Yano searched again, Riley shouted, "You said Copeland wouldn't be there!"

"What's the fun in that?" Yano grinned.

In the front, Blake cursed. "Give me a belt or something to stop the flow."

"How 'bout a zip-tie," Seth suggested.

Riley didn't care if Blake bled to death. They'd murdered a police officer. Still crying, she pleaded, "Please let me go. I don't want to hurt anyone."

"It's too late for that." Yano tapped Blake. "Let me see the wound."

Blake shifted to show the bleeding gouge across his upper arm.

Riley closed her eyes. The sight of blood gushing from the detective's throat played in her head, and she couldn't stop crying. In that dark place in her past, she had hurt someone… and there had been a lot of blood.

Chapter 32

The Old Life

He sounded so much like his dad

Three years earlier (flashback)

Riley stared at the pink line showing in the white plastic tube. She was pregnant! A cacophony of emotions flooded her. Joy, fear, love, and worry. It was too soon. They weren't ready. How had it even happened? She'd been taking her pills… except that one day she missed. *Oh hell.* Maybe it was meant to be. She'd wanted a baby for so long and just hadn't found the right guy until Luke. Joy won out and Riley squealed. A happy dance seized control of her body and she laughed with delight. Tuck whined at the door, and she let him in.

"You're gonna be a big brother!" He wagged his tail at her excitement. She hoped Luke would feel the same.

What if he didn't?

He would be worried about money. And now she was too. When she started showing, she'd have to quit her job. No one wanted a pregnant woman serving them drinks, reminding them of how toxic alcohol was. She couldn't wait to give notice. Serving alcohol disgusted her, and she was sick of men harassing her, commenting on her looks, her breasts, her clothes. Oh, but the money! Sometimes drunk men just walked up and handed her twenty-dollar bills, saying, "This is for the dress." Where else could she make an average of forty or fifty bucks an hour?

It didn't matter. Going forward, her job would be to mother this child…*and* to be a good role model. No more helping people get drunk in bars. Riley wanted to tell Luke right away, but she would wait and see what kind of mood he came home in.

She skipped into the kitchen and started prepping his favorite meal. A few minutes later, she heard the door open, so she stepped into the living room. "Hi, babe."

Luke shrugged off his coat, his face distressed.

"Rough day?" She scooted over and kissed him. "I'm making your favorite, pot roast and mashed taters. Then we can watch a movie later."

"Nice." His tone was flat.

"That bad, huh?" She moved back toward the kitchen and eased him along with her. "Tell me what happened."

"Just more of the same." He grabbed a beer from the fridge and downed half. "Students out of control, followed by angry parents who don't want them sent home."

"You gotta find another job, hon. I don't need to have health insurance." That was no longer true. Still, she felt bad that Luke had stayed at the school mostly for the benefits. Considering her new condition, it was probably good that he had. "I've got something—"

"I've got a serious thing to talk about."

They'd spoken at the same time. Riley decided her announcement could wait. "What is it?"

"The project I mentioned Dad lined up for me? He needs us both."

Oh fuck. Riley ground her teeth to keep from bitching at him. "I told you; I don't want to be involved."

Luke gulped more beer. "It's not optional."

He sounded so much like his dad in that moment, she felt a little freaked out. "Hey, don't go all Yano on me."

"Sorry." Luke pulled her in and kissed her neck. "I love you, babe."

Riley stiffened, refusing to let herself be distracted by her intense physical attraction to him. "I have to finish making dinner." She pulled back and stepped over to the counter, where she'd been prepping green beans.

"We don't have time. You can eat the leftover Thai food and I'll make myself a sandwich."

A new sense of dread. "What do you mean? Time for what?"

"We're doing it tonight and we have to meet Yano soon."

Oh god. "You told him I would participate?" Riley shook her head and her whole body shuddered.

Luke reached for her again. "Just this once, babe. I promise. The payout will be huge and we need the money. As you said, I have to quit teaching."

"But why me? Yano has a whole stable of people—"

"It's all set up for tonight, but Lexi got in a fight with her boyfriend and took off. So Dad needs both of us to step in." Luke stroked her hair. "We owe him for the down payment. Then we'll be free… of everything."

Riley felt herself wavering, moments away from giving in to Luke and his family again. She wanted to stand firm, but the money and the chance to change their lives was so tempting. Their baby needed parents who were happy, not people who hated their jobs. "How much is the payout?"

"It should be seventy thousand or so for the car, then a personal injury payout to each of us for thirty or forty grand. Even minus Dad's cut, we'll net a hundred or more."

Damn. That was hard to turn down. "If I do this, you'll find a new job? No more stalling?"

"I swear on my life." He grinned and crossed his heart.

"What do I have to do?"

"I'll let Dad fill you in." Luke hugged her hard. "Thank you."

A half hour later, they pulled into an empty lot next to a closed home-improvement store. Luke drove to the edge of the clearing and parked under a canopy of maple trees. They had crossed the Tacoma city line and were on the outskirts of Parkland. As her eyes adjusted to the dark scene, Riley realized another car sat nearby. An old compact similar to her own ancient Toyota.

"Let's trade seats." Luke opened his door.

"What? Why do I have to drive?"

"It's safer."

Right. The passenger was always more at risk in an accident. "But I don't know what to do. I'm not prepared."

Luke patted her arm. "Don't worry. Yano's a pro at this. Just let him handle it."

Riley's pulse jumped and she tried to reassure herself. Luke wouldn't let her do this if it was dangerous. As she took her place behind the wheel, Yano drove up in a small SUV she'd never seen before. As the owner of a used car lot, he drove a different vehicle every week. Riley was surprised to see Donna in the passenger seat. Her mother-in-law stayed put while Yano strode over, wearing a dark tracksuit that made him nearly invisible except for his pale face. An oversized, messenger-style bag was strapped across his chest.

Riley rolled down her window, and Luke's cousin, JT, got out of the other compact car and joined them.

"Hi Riley. Luke." He sounded nervous.

"Here's the basic plan," Yano said, his voice quiet and conspiratorial. "I'll be driving the at-fault car." He pointed at the Nissan JT had arrived in. "And I'll handle the crash." He grabbed Riley's face with both hands. "All you have to do is let it happen. I'll be comin' at you fast, but don't brake or jerk the wheel." He kissed her on the mouth. "You can do this, girl. And thanks, by the way, for filling in. Looney Lexi has let me down before."

Oh fuckity fuck. Riley's anxiety mounted. *This was crazy.*

Yano clapped his nephew's shoulder. "Our at-fault driver. Let's hear your line again."

JT shoved his hands in his pockets. "I dropped my water bottle and when I reached for it, my shoulder musta hit the wheel. And I lost control."

Yano pivoted to Riley. "All you have to say is the truth. Another car just suddenly swerved toward you."

Riley's stomach churned and she was glad she hadn't eaten. She wanted to run from this insanity. She stared at JT, feeling less affectionate for him. "Have you done this before?"

"Not since Phoenix. And I was the victim that time." He tried to smile. "So this will be easy in comparison."

She glanced at Luke, but he wouldn't meet her eyes. Her husband had done this previously too, before they met, and hadn't told her. His deceit cut into her heart. What else was he hiding? *Don't think about that now. Just be glad everyone knew what they were doing.* This would turn out okay and the settlement would give her and Luke their freedom. A fresh start. No secrets.

Yano handed her a neck brace. "Put this on."

Fingers trembling, Riley latched the velcro as Yano reached across her and handed Luke a brace too.

Luke shook his head. "This car is too old to have airbags. I need a helmet."

"Don't be a pussy." Yano scoffed and shook his head. "I didn't bring one. Just put the brace on."

"After the next part."

Riley spun toward him. "After the accident? That makes no sense."

"I mean after we create the claim injuries." Luke grimaced. "Brace yourself and look at Dad."

What? Riley turned to Yano. He pulled a brick from his shoulder bag and smashed it into her forehead.

The pain was blinding. "What the fuck?"

"Shh." Yano reached into his carryall again and handed her a plastic bottle filled with a dark-yellow liquid.

"Is that pee?" Her forehead throbbed so hard she could barely focus.

"Yeah. Dump it on your pants. It'll look like you passed out and pissed yourself."

Riley gave Luke her most scathing stare. He blinked hard and mouthed *I love you.*

She turned back in time to see Yano hit JT on the jaw with the brick. He silently rubbed the wound, but Yano was agitated. "Damn. That's not bleeding enough. Here, take this sandpaper to it." He dug in his bag.

Fuckity fuck. Riley took deep breaths. This was a whole staged production.

Now her father-in-law scurried to her husband's side of the car and gashed his brow with a boxcutter. "Take this aspirin to make it bleed more." Matter of fact, like he'd said it a dozen times before.

So much pain and trauma and they hadn't even been in the accident yet. No wonder Luke hadn't wanted to share any details. He knew she would have refused. She still could. Riley got out of the Lexus, leaving the key in the ignition. If Luke wanted to do this, she wouldn't try to stop him. But she was out.

"Hey!" Yano and Luke called to her at the same time.

She stepped toward JT and pleaded. "Will you drive me home?"

"I would love to, but I can't. I'm sorry."

Yano grabbed Riley's arm and walked her toward the trees. "Do you love my son?"

He was playing the guilt card, straight up. "You know I do."

"Then you know he's unhappy. This is your chance to help him." He squeezed her arm. "Luke just needs thirty minutes of your time. Can you spare that, Riley?"

She jerked free. "Don't act like you're doing this for Luke. You make money from every accident you stage."

"And I share that money with my family," he hissed, spittle flying. "Vacations, low-cost nice cars, and the occasional mortgage down payment." He stepped toward her, his voice a low-pitched snarl. "Remember that? You owe me. Now get your ass into that car and stop being such a *prima donna.*"

Riley seethed, chewing the inside of her cheek until it bled. There was nothing left to say and no one to drive her home. She was trapped and it was her own fault. Walking in the dark rain until she could find a ride seemed riskier too. And with no pay-off. *Oh fuck it.* His family and friends wouldn't keep doing this if anyone had ever gotten seriously hurt. She pushed past Yano, strode to the Lexus, and got back behind the wheel.

Luke reached for her, but she brushed him off.

Through the window, Yano shoved a Red Bull into Riley's hands. "Drink half and give the rest to Luke. We need your blood pressure to spike for the paramedics."

"That won't be a problem." She choked out a harsh laugh. Her head already felt like it would explode.

Yano reached across her again and handed a small burner phone to Luke. "We'll stay in contact about traffic and timing."

"I know." Her husband's voice was tight.

"Same location we talked about. Halfway down the slope on South Hill Drive." Yano cocked his head at Riley.

"Got it." She couldn't look at him.

"I think we're ready." Yano—the bastard freak!—sounded cheerful, like a man headed to a tailgating party. He spun toward JT and held out his hand for a key. "See you all shortly." Yano trotted over to the Nissan and got behind the wheel. Now Riley thought she understood. He was going to crash that car into hers. But somehow, JT would take the blame.

Luke's cousin patted her arm, then got into Yano's car with Donna.

For a moment, Riley was confused again about how it would play out, then realized Yano and JT would switch again after the crash.

Luke finally put on his neck brace. "Riley, I swear to you,

after we get the insurance payments, we'll quit our jobs, sell the house, and move anywhere you want."

Her throat was too tight to respond.

A light rain fell as they drove east, and Riley had second thoughts. "Maybe we should wait—"

"No. It's fine." Luke went back to listening to his dad on the burner cell.

She could hear Yano's voice through the speakerphone, but she couldn't process what he was saying. None of it was important to her anyway. She just had to drive where she was told and not flinch when the time came.

Two more turns into a rural area with little housing. At the top of a gentle slope, Luke told her to pull over and wait. She leaned back and tried to think happy thoughts, but the pain in her forehead was getting worse and caffeine was pulsing in her veins. How was she supposed to concentrate? "I don't think I can do this."

Luke covered the burner phone's speaker. "All you have to do is drive. Any moment now."

The rain on the windshield was now a steady staccato. Riley told herself it didn't matter. She'd grown up in Washington, the wettest place in the country. This was just another evening.

"Let's go." Luke signaled her like a race car coach.

She pressed the accelerator and eased onto the road.

Halfway down the slope, headlights came at her. *This was it.*

Her heartbeat escalated as the other vehicle gained speed.

"Shit!" Yano was going too fast!

"Steady!" Luke snapped.

Riley tightened her grip on the wheel and the headlights screamed toward her.

At the last moment, they swerved into her lane. Thunder boomed at the same time and Riley panicked, instinctively steering away from the oncoming car.

But she turned too far and they careened off the road.

"No!" Luke shouted.

Riley hit the brakes, but it was too late. The right side of the car slammed into a tree. The impact threw her forward, then slammed her back into the seat. As the car spun, her mind went blank.

Moments later, she woke to Yano shouting and running toward her. "Stupid bitch! You weren't supposed to avoid me."

Riley touched her painful forehead, then realized the injury wasn't from the crash, but from the brick Yano had struck her with. She was okay.

She turned to Luke. And screamed. His side of the car was crumpled, and her beautiful husband was a bloody mess. "No! No! Nooo!"

She struggled to unbuckle her seatbelt, desperate to help him.

Yano yanked open her car door. "We can still file a claim. Give me the neck braces and the phone so I can get out of here."

"Luke is really hurt!" She screamed, rage and fear funneling into the projectile that was now her voice.

"Shit." Yano hustled around to the passenger side, but he couldn't open the crumpled door. "Call 911!"

Riley was shaking so hard she couldn't get her seatbelt loose, let alone find her phone.

But Yano was shouting at JT, who stood by her open door, staring in shock.

"You're bleeding." He pulled his phone as he moved toward her.

Riley looked down at her lap. That wasn't just bottled urine. It was blood, flowing like an ugly period. She started to cry, then sob, her body heaving so hard she thought it would break. This was her stupid fault! Why couldn't she have been hurt instead of her precious family?

Chapter 33

The Old Life
Just tell the truth

Two days later (flashback)

Riley stared at the muted TV but didn't process the images. She was lying in a hospital bed, floating in a cloud of medication, unaware of time, and too depressed to function. What was the point? Luke was dead. Their baby gone.

A psychologist had visited her twice, but their conversations had been short and pointless. *Did she have suicidal thoughts?* Of course! She'd driven off the road into a tree and killed them both. If she knew a quick and easy way to end her own life she would do it. But everything she considered took planning and energy, and she didn't have any. She also couldn't bear the thought of going home to the house Luke no longer lived in. She needed someone to sell it for her and give Yano his blood money back. But she didn't trust anyone and didn't want to talk to anyone she knew. Guilt and shame were like parasites, eating what was left of the fragile fabric of her existence. If she lay here long enough, she would simply cease to exist.

But the nurses wouldn't let her. They kept getting her up, making her walk, and changing the bandages on her forehead.

Yano would be pleased to know his brick slam had paid off, and her head injury had shown up on a CT. Her friends wouldn't leave her alone either. JT and Trina had both tried to visit, but Riley had told the nurses no. Her mother hadn't bothered, and Riley wasn't surprised. They still hadn't spoken since their big fight, but they'd been in conflict before that, mostly over each other's boyfriends. But now that Riley had been involved in insurance fraud and committed manslaughter, her mother might never speak to her again.

A shuffling sound made her look up. An older man in a gray suit was in the doorway. "I'm Detective Copeland, Tacoma Police. I need to ask you some questions."

She'd known this moment was coming. Yesterday's nurse had turned away a uniform cop before he'd reached her door. But stalling was pointless. She was ready. In fact, she hoped he would arrest her. She couldn't stay in the hospital much longer and she couldn't go home. Jail seemed like the best place, a punishment she deserved.

"Sure." She sat up, wishing she had on real clothes instead of this stupid gown. She was tired of the sling on her arm too.

A second man stepped in behind the first. He was tall, handsome, and wore a black turtleneck.

"This is Detective Becker."

Riley nodded, feeling intimidated.

The older guy walked over to stand beside her bed. "What made you drive off the road?"

Her nurse, a young guy with tattoos, barged in. "My patient is grieving. This can wait."

Riley held up her hand. "It's okay. I need to get through this."

The nurse glared and stayed in the doorway. The taller detective slid the folding door closed in his face.

Copeland repeated the question, then added, "There were no skid marks. You didn't even brake." His voice was gentle, but his dark eyes seemed to burn through her.

Riley's throat felt sticky and she reached for her water.

"Were you trying to kill yourself?" Copeland pressed.

"No." She swallowed hard.

"Was there another car on the road?"

Riley nodded. "We were trying to commit insurance fraud."

His eyes widened and he pulled out a recorder. "I need to document this."

"Okay." Where to start? And who to blame? She took another gulp of water. *Just tell the truth*, her mother used to say. So she did. "Here's what happened. My father-in-law, Aden Sebastiano, was driving what he calls the *at-fault* car. He was coming straight at me, and his wife, Donna Mackey, was with him. I was supposed to just let him crash into me, but I panicked." The horrifying moment played in her mind, and tears welled in Riley's eyes. "It was raining, then I heard thunder, and my instinct was to swerve. I mean, who wouldn't?" She fought for control. "Unlike the others, I'd never done it before. And I didn't want to." She was crying now, hating herself. "But they pressured me."

Copeland finally sat and opened a small notepad. Becker remained standing, his face unreadable.

"Take a moment to calm yourself," the older man said, "then start at the beginning."

After describing her involvement, from the moment they'd accepted the down payment, Riley felt lighter, free of the burden of carrying secrets. But Copeland wasn't done. "What do you know about Yano's car-theft racket?"

The question caught her off guard, but nothing about her amoral father-in-law could shock her now. "Not a thing. I swear. I didn't even know about the insurance scams until they asked me to play a victim." That wasn't totally true, but close enough.

"The car you were driving was likely stolen from the airport's long-term parking last year."

Oh no.

Copeland narrowed his eyes at her. "But the VIN was damaged so we can't be certain yet. Do you know anything about how it got damaged?"

"No." Riley fought back more tears. Had Luke known about the theft? Had she ever really known him? "As I told you, my husband bought the car from Yano's dealership a few months ago. I had no idea it was stolen."

Becker, the tall guy, cut in. "How did you pay for it?"

"I'm not certain. Luke just said Yano gave him a great deal."

"I'm sure." Copeland smiled wryly. "Did you ever hear Yano mention a partner?"

"I really didn't spend much time with him." Riley's phone blasted an ominous sound. *Oh no.* The ringtone she'd set up for Yano. "That's him calling me now." She reached over and pressed Reject.

"No!" Copeland scowled. "We need to hear what he says. Has he tried to intimidate you?"

"I haven't answered." Yano had called twice and she'd forgotten to block his number. "I never want to hear his voice again. Or speak to him."

"That's understandable." Copeland locked eyes on her. "If he tries to silence you or threatens you in any way, please contact me immediately." He held out a business card. "We've had an open investigation into Sebastiano's activities for a while, and I'm now leading it. When you're ready, I'd like to bring you in and have you look at some photos, see if you recognize anyone in connection with him."

Riley took the card. "Will I be arrested?"

"Yes. I'll do that before I leave, so you can be arraigned. The court will notify you of when to appear."

"You're not taking me to jail?"

"No. I'm sure the DA will offer you a plea deal if you agree to cooperate and testify against the others."

He meant Yano, JT, and Donna. She hated to turn on Luke's cousin—poor JT had probably been sucked in with debts and favors like they had—but Riley would gladly tighten the screws on the power couple. Their greed, combined with her own weakness, had ruined her life.

Chapter 34

The Turbulent Present
Can't do a damn thing to stop us

Sept. 10, Tacoma (day 3 after the kidnapping)

After a long day of working leads and freeway driving, Dallas parked in the back lot of the Tacoma Police Department. This might be her last work stop, but she still needed to find a room and read through the paperwork she'd picked up at the prison. First, she took a moment to eat the chicken sandwich she'd bought, then washed it down with lukewarm, sweetened coffee. Eating healthy was a priority at home, but when she worked undercover or went on the road, the rules went out the window. She wiped her hands and checked her face in the rearview mirror. No mayo or crumbs, but most of her makeup had worn off.

Dallas got out and locked the Kia, then laughed. Even at dusk, it should be safe next to a two-story building filled with cops. For lack of a better plan, she hoped to talk to the detective who'd led the investigation into the Sebastiano family's crimes. He might be gone for the day, but many law enforcement people worked late… and often nonstop… and being one of those people herself, she wasn't ready to call it a night.

The desk officers sat behind a massive counter topped with plexiglass and both were dealing with citizens. Dallas waited, pacing and bouncing on her feet. She considered calling Copeland, but her contact info might be outdated and phones were easy to ignore. She'd always had more success with in-person requests anyway. Being an attractive woman in a male-dominated world had its advantages. Right now, she hoped to deal with the older guy behind the counter, instead of the thirty-something woman, if for no other reason than the woman was already agitated by the jackass who kept insisting she take the bail money he was offering. The other citizen left first, and Dallas stepped up to the speaker embedded in the clear shield.

"Agent Dallas, from the Phoenix bureau. I'd like to speak with Detective Copeland." She pushed her badge into the tray under the plexiglass. The desk officer—B. Gallison, according to his nametag—didn't return her smile. "What's your interest?"

"I worked the Sebastiano case when they operated in Phoenix, then came up to consult with the taskforce that investigated their activities here."

"So you know Copeland?" The desk officer's bushy eyebrows conveyed skepticism

"Yes."

"Then you should know he retired."

Oh hell. "I shouldn't be surprised, but I haven't spoken to him since our work together years ago." Feeling weary, she transferred her heavy bag to the other shoulder. "But I'm looking into new developments in the case. Will you give me his contact information?"

"Let me see what I can find." Gallison spent a minute searching digital files. "I've got Copeland's phone number. Ready?"

Dallas pulled her cell and keyed in the info as he recited it. "What about an address?"

The desk officer shook his head. "You'll have to get that from him."

She didn't have time to play phone tag. "What if he doesn't pick up my call because he doesn't recognize my number? I'm looking for a missing woman, so my investigation is critical and timely. I need to see him ASAP."

Gallison nodded, finally on board. "I'll try to reach Copeland for you."

While he made the call, Dallas checked her email. A sweet message from Cameron, but nothing from her boss. The door behind her opened and two young men walked in. She tried to guess their issue. Stolen property or a problem with their landlord.

Gallison cleared his throat. "Copeland isn't answering." He wrote something on a slip of paper and pushed it through the tray.

Dallas picked it up. Copeland's address!

"It's in Lakeland South."

"Thanks." She would visit him first thing in the morning. Tonight, she had to read through Yano's correspondence with his incarcerated wife. Maybe if she found something interesting, the detective would have useful insight.

She found a hotel halfway between the department and Copeland's address and told the desk clerk she needed a couple of nights. In her room, Dallas showered, then lay down for a few minutes, not caring about the amenities. The last three days had been a whirlwind of activity and she needed to recharge. The Wendy's coffee had given her anxiety, but not much energy.

After fifteen minutes, Dallas made herself get up and open the folder of letters and digital printouts. Sitting in bed, she skimmed through them. Most of Donna's texts referenced visiting days and hours, while Yano's were badly written summaries of mundane activities:... *bought a new laptop... hired a landscaper to plant a privacy hedge... cashed out an annuity.*

The last one, dated two months earlier, was moderately interesting. A signal that Yano was liquidating assets. Now that his wife was free, but wanted, they might be headed out of the country. But without specifics, the information wasn't particularly helpful. Under the stack of text printouts were two letters. The first, written years earlier, mentioned Yano's move to Toledo to be near the prison, including a rant about how he *missed his real house* and would *never forgive the petty people* who had taken it from him.

Criminals with grudges often sought revenge. Kidnapping, and possibly killing Riley Brockwell fit that scenario. Brockwell had effectively put a stop to his scams and forced him to spend thousands on criminal defense lawyers. The bank had eventually foreclosed on his property. Why hadn't he just sold it? Most people who got themselves into a foreclosure position were either lazy or depressed or dysfunctional in some way. But she suspected with Yano the issue was ego. He hadn't been able to admit defeat or willingly let go of a prize he thought he deserved.

Now he'd helped his wife escape from prison. Was he stupid enough to think they could lay low and hide out at his new place, wherever it was? She'd searched county files all over Washington and hadn't found any property in his or Donna's names, and continuing to search could be pointless. Yano could have bought the house under a business name. Or a phony charity. Still, the question remained: What did he plan next? Flee the country with his fugitive wife? Or carry out more revenge?

Megalomaniacs were unpredictable.

Dallas got up to pace, realizing there was a secondary question: *Why now?*

On the surface, that seemed easy. The same reason she'd started her investigation. Riley's dog, Tuck, had appeared in a news story, and Yano had tracked her down. Yet the prison escape may have already been in the planning stages. The warden had said his work-crew schedules were based on county and state needs and could change at the last moment. But overall, they followed seasonal patterns of cleanup: weed and blackberry spraying in the spring and campsite maintenance in late summer and fall. During their in-person visits, Donna had likely conveyed specific information about where she would be.

Dallas sat back down and read through the messages again. A line in a text from three months earlier now stood out. Yano had casually mentioned a doctor's appointment. Sometimes, medical scares motivated people to make lifestyle changes—or to make the most of the time they had left. Which brought her back to a similar question: Was Yano spending more time with his wife or plotting more revenge?

Exhausted, Dallas decided to call Cameron, then get some sleep. He didn't pick up. She was both disappointed and relieved. She wanted to hear his deep soothing voice, to be reminded that he loved her and would be there for her when she got home. But she was also too tired to be a decent conversationalist and had no idea when she would make it back to Arizona.

An hour after she zonked out, her phone beeped with an email message. Thinking it might be Cameron checking in after finishing a bartending shift, she sat up and looked at it. Yano had emailed her at her work address, his first contact since the taskforce had disbanded. The taunting tone was familiar: *Dizzy (but gorgeous) Dallas. I think about you a lot, especially when I'm horny. You did your best to sabotage me with your bullshit investigation, but it wasn't good enough. Now Donna is free too and we're living the good life. Or we will be soon. Too bad you're in Phoenix and can't do a damn thing to stop us. Adios!*

Good thing the man's ego overrode his limited intellectual abilities. She now knew he was headed to Mexico. But not quite yet. She sensed he had something else to take care of. Yano also didn't know she was right on his tail. Dallas forwarded the email to the bureau's technicians. Maybe they could track the IP address and help her locate him. She suspected his unfinished business was here in the Seattle-Tacoma area, where his criminal empire had fallen apart.

In the morning, she would call Agent Saul Wheeler in the Seattle bureau. He'd eventually joined the taskforce too, and she was curious to know if Yano had contacted him as well. The thing that still puzzled her was how Yano knew she'd been on the taskforce. She'd come in as an undercover agent and had never interviewed the ringleader, either in Phoenix or Tacoma. She'd watched a couple of his sessions, so she felt like she knew him. But how did he know her? The rumors about how well connected he was had always been about his ability to get access and information. But what if his connections went deeper than that?

Chapter 35

The Turbulent Present
They all worked against him

Around the same time

Too wound up to sleep, Yano checked his Ameritrade account for Genovics' price. Already over two hundred. Sweet! If he sold right now, he'd net a quick fifty grand. But the stock was still rising, so he'd let it go for another day or so, then cash out. Donna would need every dollar he could scrape together. He got up, poured himself a finger of bourbon, then took it back to bed. He'd spent a lot of nights like this recently, just him, his iPad, and a smooth drink. But he'd soon have his wife by his side again.

Feeling upbeat, he checked his list of everyone who'd wronged him. Organized by categories, he'd hoped to work through everyone, but he was running out of time. The cancer had spread, and he might only have a year left. Spending time with Donna was his priority—along with drinking margaritas on the beach—but he had one more project to pull off in the morning before he joined her.

He re-read the text he'd just sent Dallas, his favorite fed. He'd thought about adding her to his terminate list, but she was too gorgeous and too crafty. All that beauty and talent wasted as a cop. She'd come on to JT back in Phoenix, trying to seduce him for info, but Yano hadn't been fooled. As soon as he'd laid eyes on her, he'd known she was too good for his nephew. So he'd checked with his inside man and sure enough, the local cops and feds were onto him. But that was the life. Pack up and move every five or seven years to stay ahead of the sting. He liked to stir things up anyway.

Who else should he text just to fuck with? Copeland was already dead, the ring back in his possession. The other two detectives who'd wronged him, Becker and Silva, were all set for payback in the morning. That left Saul Wheeler, the other federal agent who'd been on the persecution team. Yano started a message to Wheeler, then changed his mind. Wheeler was boring and pointless, not a star player. Yano set aside his tablet, pulled down his boxers, and stroked his penis until he was hard, which took longer than it used to. The cancer, the chemo, the booze—which he wasn't supposed to have—plus physical inactivity, they all worked against him. He snapped a photo, then sent the dick pic to Dallas just for fun.

Yano chuckled at the thought of Blake, Seth, and Riley all sleeping on the other side of the wall. Their last night together in a motel suite. He got up and wandered to the window, opened the drapes, and stared at the night lights. He loved the Sea-Tac area and had missed it. When he'd lived here, his affection and complacency had become a problem. He'd known it was time to relocate, but his boys had both gotten married and didn't want to move again. Two of Donna's girls had settled down as well. They could've restarted the business without the kids, but he didn't like to depend on outsiders. So he'd stayed, then everything had gone to shit and he'd lost Luke. So tragic and avoidable.

Fuck! Yano spun and threw his bourbon glass against the wall. They all had to pay.

Chapter 36

The Turbulent Present
That idea had been delusional

Sept. 11, Tacoma (day 4 after the kidnapping)

Riley lay on the floor of a motel room, using a towel for a blanket. Yano slept in a separate bedroom, and his thugs were taking turns napping in the main bed and watching the door. She assumed they were concerned with keeping her in and the cops out. Anxiety—and Yano's weird noises—had kept her awake half the night, but at least she had Tuck with her, his radiant body feeding her energy and love. Yano had made good on his half-assessed promise to reward her by letting doggo snuggle with her for a while.

She had no idea what they planned next, but every possibility terrified her. They'd killed a retired police officer, and she suspected they'd intended to all along. Now that some of her *old life* memories had come back, Yano's violence rather surprised her. He hadn't been like that when she'd known him before. Or had he? He'd risked his family members' lives for luxury money. She no longer trusted anyone to be who they said they were. Luke had betrayed her. Yano had turned on her. And even Thomas had turned out to be sketchy.

A beeping sound woke her from a half-dream state in which she'd been trying to escape a maze with weights on her ankles. Riley sat up, confused by the proximity of a wall and a bed.

Yano's voice cut through her fog. "Everybody up. The big day is finally here."

Riley latched her bra, slipped on her Sketchers, then gathered Tuck into her arms and stood. Now that he was free from the cage, was this their chance? They were on the ground floor and the window was a slider that actually opened.

"Don't even think about it," Yano warned. He eased around the end of the bed and yanked Tuck from her grip. "Use the bathroom real quick if you need to, cuz this is your last chance." His chipper tone didn't soften the ominous words.

Riley moved past Blake as he pulled on his jeans, then went into the bathroom and locked the door. At least they hadn't raped her. She worried about it every time she lay down and closed her eyes with these thugs nearby.

In the mirror, her face seemed paler and thinner than she remembered. The makeup she'd put on yesterday morning for the prison break—had that been only yesterday?—was gone except for some smeared mascara. She wanted to shower, but Yano had said "quick," and the lock wouldn't keep any of them out. They still had the drill and a duffle bag full of other stuff that made her nervous. Riley splashed cold water on her face, washed her pits with a wet washrag, and rinsed her teeth as best she could. Even if this was her last day on earth, she wanted some dignity. *Ha!* She was still wearing the sexy hooker shorts and camisole under sweatpants and a hoodie. *So classy!*

A fist pounded on the bathroom door. "Let's go."

She pulled in a deep breath and stepped out.

"Shove your hands in the pouch," Blake commanded.

She complied, and he managed to secure her wrists with zip-ties while they were inside the pocket, masking her captivity. Blake passed her to Seth, who walked her out of the motel. No one watching would have guessed she was a prisoner, but in the early predawn light, no other guests were in the parking lot. Yano and Blake followed, carrying more duffle bags, plus Tuck's cage, and they all climbed into the 4Runner again.

They drove west to a storage place on the other side of Swan Creek Park. The business took up several acres and sat between an outdoor miniature golf course that hadn't opened yet for the day and a home improvement store that had gone out of business. Seth, behind the wheel again, stopped at the security post, punched in a code, and the gate rolled open. Halide lamps over the front office cast a harsh light on the rows of narrow metal buildings with hundreds of units. Seth zigzagged through the rows to a far corner and parked in front of a large storage space near the end. Riley assumed they were here to retrieve something.

She was wrong.

"I'll get started on the fence." Seth scurried to the back of the vehicle.

Riley glanced over her shoulder to see him pull long-handled bolt cutters from a duffle bag. He strode to the ten-foot, chain-link fence and started snipping. Blake yanked her out of the vehicle and walked her to the storage unit. Yano set down a black briefcase, opened the padlock, and rolled up the metal overhead door. The dark space was empty except for a chair and a small folding table.

This was where they would torture and kill her.

Dread flooded Riley's body and her legs buckled. She landed knees first on the concrete floor, too pain-shocked to move. Blake grabbed her hair and dragged her to the chair while Yano turned on a light and closed the overhead door.

Riley wanted to plead for them to end her life quickly, but she had nothing left. No energy, no will to live. Now that she remembered her part in Luke's death, guilt had become her overriding emotion again. She deserved to die. Tuck didn't deserve his fate, but she had to accept that she had no control over it. That idea had been delusional.

"Get up," Blake snapped.

Riley couldn't move.

He yanked her onto the chair, secured her to the back with an extension cord, then reached in her pouch pocket and freed her hands.

"You have to make a call." Yano's expression held the hint of a juicy secret.

"To who?"

"Detective Becker."

A chill crawled up Riley's spine. "And say what?"

"That you have evidence you want to turn over. Tell him you're tired of hiding."

None of this made sense. "I don't want anyone else to get hurt."

"He won't." Yano squeezed her cheeks. "Just tell him to come to Pioneer Storage, unit eight-six." He handed her a burner phone with a number keyed in. "Do this for me, and I'll let your dog go. I promise."

Riley wanted to believe him. He hadn't harmed Tuck and almost seemed to have some affection for doggo. She also wasn't worried about Becker, even if this was a trap. *Why not?* The thought surprised her.

Blake pointed a gun at her head.

"Do it." Yano reached over and pressed the Call icon.

While the phone rang, Riley tried to form the right words, but she was too rattled to think straight.

The detective answered on the third ring, sounded annoyed. "Becker."

"Uhh. It's Riley Brockwell and I'm tired of hiding." She pulled in a breath. "If you want the evidence, come to Pioneer Storage, unit eighty-six."

A long silence. "When?"

"Now."

Yano reached over and ended the call. "Well done. Now take off your sweatshirt."

They were gonna beat her. Was there any point in resisting? If she did, someone would hit her in the face again, then punch her torso anyway. Riley pulled off the hoodie, her old friend anger starting to surface. Blake tossed the garment aside.

Yano opened the briefcase he'd carried in and took out a heavy canvas vest. He held it out for her. "Look what I got you."

Oh mother of god. It was a bomb with what looked like five sticks of dynamite wired together. But they could be any kind of explosive. Riley began to shake. What if she screamed? Was anyone close enough to hear and call for help? *No.* They'd chosen this location for a reason. Yano would just assault and gag her, then tape the bomb to her anyway. She was a dead woman walking. "Please don't make me hurt anyone with that."

"Just a couple of cops who deserve it."

"Please don't," Riley begged. "I'll help you with other projects, whatever you want."

"Shh. I need to focus." Yano laid the vest on the table. "I have to rig both the timer and the detonator." He glanced over with a devilish grin. "With the detonator, we can blow you up at any point. The timer is just a backup, to make sure you all go kaboom even if I have to skedaddle for some reason."

Riley closed her eyes. She couldn't stop this. "Please don't kill Tuck."

"If everything goes according to plan, I'll drop him off on my way out of town." Yano laughed. "Now be still and quiet while I rig this."

Riley wanted to close her eyes, but she had one last hope. So she watched what Yano was doing, glancing away often enough that he wouldn't notice her attention.

He pulled an icepick from his tool case and dug a deep but skinny hole in the middle stick of explosive. The next thing he handled was hard to see, but it looked like a two-inch plastic cylinder about the diameter of a pencil with a wire sticking out one end. Yano surprised her by taking gum from his mouth and attaching a portion of it to the other end of the weird tube. Then he pushed the cylinder into the hole he'd made.

The detonator. Riley understood that much about bombs. You needed the explosive—the sticks, whatever they were made of—and some other chemical to set them off.

Yano turned to her with a fake smile. "Patience."

A flash of hatred burned through her numbness, distracting her with a brief fantasy about grabbing Blake's gun and shooting them both. But he'd moved too far away. She forced herself to stay focused and keep watching. Remembering this process wouldn't be as easy as recalling words, but she had to try.

From his tool bag, Yano extracted a strange-looking contraption attached to a cell phone. The device was a flat, four-inch piece of beige plastic perforated with holes. Stuck to it were circuit components and wires connecting to the phone. Short red and black ones on one end and what looked like a white charger cord on the other.

She didn't know the names or functions of the little components, but she understood how Yano would set off the bomb—by calling the phone/device and sending an electrical charge to the detonator.

Her last hope evaporated.

"This is the tricky part," Yano muttered.

Riley gritted her teeth, watching as he carefully attached the explosive's wire to one end of the plastic base. Red and black wires stuck out of something at the other end and were somehow attached to the cell.

"The phone is also the timer," Yano said, sounding pleased with himself. "I think an hour should be plenty." He tucked the device into an empty sleeve on the vest. "It's amazing what you can learn on the dark web if you have the time." He picked up the rigged vest by its shoulder straps "Arms up."

Riley couldn't make herself move.

Yano dug a thumb into her eye. "I said 'arms up.'"

Tears rolling down one side of her face, she did what she was told. Yano carefully tugged the vest down over her shoulders, then handed her the sweatshirt. "Put it back on."

Riley shook so hard she thought she might set off the explosive. She wished she could. Blowing up this psychopath with his own bomb would be poetic justice.

"Put your hands back in the pouch."

Motherfucker.

Blake reached in and zip-tied her wrists again, leaving her no possibility of disassembling the bomb.

Riley felt like she couldn't breathe, as if she would suffocate to death. The sensation triggered another wave of memories.

Chapter 37

The Old Life
He's an obsessive type

Two years and four months earlier (flashback)

As she sat down to eat dinner, a wave of depression hit her. Alone, in a tiny apartment with no Luke and no baby. All she had in this life was a job she hated and the threat of going to jail if she didn't keep testifying. JT had taken a plea deal and was already incarcerated, but Donna was fighting her charges in court, and Yano was stalling, filing motion after motion.

Not hungry, Riley put her salad in the fridge, then heard Tuck whine. Feeling guilty for not counting his wonderful presence in her life, she picked him up for a snuggle. "That was just lettuce and stuff. You wouldn't have liked it."

To get out of her funk, she cranked up her tunes and danced for forty minutes. Tuck tried to participate, as usual, then gave up and watched.

After she showered, she tried to eat again, but her phone beeped with an email message. Knowing she shouldn't, Riley checked it. This one from Donna's youngest daughter: *U selfish bitch! How dare you rat out mom. U screwed up. Just keep yr mouth shut and do the time.*

Donna's two older daughters had also called and texted until she'd blocked them. Riley reported the first few to Detective Copeland, but since no one had specifically threatened her, he couldn't do anything. Riley marked the email as spam and tried to finish her meal, but a knock at her door startled her. No one except Copeland and Trina knew where she lived now, and her best friend was working tonight. She'd sold the house months earlier and sent Yano a check for his down payment.

Riley wanted to ignore whoever it was and pretend to not be home, but Tuck was barking and trotting over. She might as well just deal with it.

At the door, she called out, "Who is it?"

"Matt."

Shit. Luke's older brother. How had he found her address? A terrifying thought. "Go away or I'll call the police."

"I come in peace with an offer you can't refuse." The Sebastiano charm oozed through the door.

What did Yano have besides money? She wouldn't make that mistake again. "Not interested."

"Tuck might be."

That hooked her, and Riley opened the door. "What's that supposed to mean?"

Matt stepped forward, forcing her back, then barged his way in. He smiled broadly, looking a lot like Luke. "Yano wants to make a sizable donation to the Jack Russell Rescue in your name."

"Great. Tell him I said thanks." Riley smirked, knowing this was all bullshit.

"So you'll be friendly with us again?"

An indirect bribe. Nothing the police or FBI could do anything about. "Just leave."

"If you decide to skip out on court, we can help you start over somewhere else."

Riley shook her head.

Matt moved toward her, his six-foot-two athletic body intimidating on its own. "Then Yano wants his ring back."

She decided to give it to him, just to be rid of the connection and the reminder of Luke's proposal. She started to tell him that.

But Matt cut her off. "Or he'll file theft charges."

The jackass! "Tell Yano I said to fuck straight off. And don't ever come here and threaten me again."

"Hey, that wasn't a threat."

Riley reached in her pocket for her phone. "I'm calling the police right now."

Matt left quickly, but she called Copeland anyway. He answered on the second ring. "Hey, Riley. You okay?"

"Yeah. Sorry to bug you so late, but Matt Sebastiano was just here with weird bribes and threats."

"I'll be right over to take your report." The detective hung up.

Copeland arrived twenty minutes later, and she saw him casually dressed in jeans and a pullover for the first time. They'd spent hours together going over everything she'd seen and heard at Yano's family gatherings, and at this point, Riley considered him a friend. Detective Becker too. Before Copeland sat down at her little table, she offered him something to drink.

"No thanks. We'll make this quick."

Riley made herself mint tea, then recounted Matt's words as best she could.

"You're right. That's not a real threat." Copeland looked disappointed. "What's the deal with the ring anyway?"

"It's a big diamond and pretty valuable. Yano bought it for his first wife, Luke's mother, then gave it to Luke for me when we got engaged." Riley sighed. "I know Yano regrets doing that because he's mentioned it a few times."

"He's an obsessive type." Copeland seemed amused "Are you keeping it to mess with him or for sentimental reasons?"

"I want to sell it for cash. I just don't know how." She'd thought about this a lot. "As soon as I'm done testifying, I plan to leave this area and start fresh somewhere else. So I could use the money."

"Can I see the ring? I might be able to help you."

That surprised her. "Sure." Riley fetched it from a secret hiding place in her closet and held it out for Copeland.

He held it to the light and whistled. "Damn, that's pretty. I'm not an expert, but it may be two carats. If so, it's worth twenty thousand or more."

As he studied the ring, she worked up the nerve to ask. "What did you mean when you said you might be able to help?"

"I could buy it from you and keep it until I retired. Call it an investment." Copeland grinned. "It would be worth it just to mess with Yano."

Riley laughed for the first since the accident. "Deal."

Chapter 38

The Old Life
Some new evidence just came up

Two years earlier (flashback)

Riley stared at the TV, but her mind wasn't on the streaming show. She was due in court tomorrow to testify against Yano, and her nerves were shot. He'd filed a motion to separate his trial from his wife's, then another motion to delay it, but his time had finally run out.

Unable to sit still, Riley went to the kitchen and stuck a bag of popcorn in the microwave. Doggo tagged along as usual. While the corn popped, she paced her small apartment, Tuck watching intently from Luke's old recliner, one of the only things she'd kept from their home.

Packing and giving away Luke's clothing had been excruciating, forcing her to accept that he no longer existed anywhere. When she'd found the handgun he'd kept from her, she'd almost used it on herself. But she'd turned it in to the police and anger had burned through her grief. Luke had kept so many secrets from her—and dragged her into his family's bullshit. Donna's daughters had walked away without a single charge and occasionally still hate-messaged her for testifying against their mother.

After this week, when she'd finished her final testimony as part of her plea agreement, Riley planned to move south and never set foot in Washington again. She'd already given notice on this place.

As she took the popcorn out, her doorbell rang. Tuck barked and she dropped the bag on the counter. No one ever came here unannounced, except that time Matt had showed up to harass her. Had Yano sent him again? Riley checked her phone to see if she'd missed a text from Trina. She hadn't.

Loud knocking this time, followed by a call out. "It's Detective Becker."

Huh. That surprised her. Riley decided to see what he wanted. With Tuck at her side, she unlocked the door and eased it open a few inches.

"Some new evidence just came up," the detective said through the crack. "And we need to discuss it before you take the stand."

"I'm too nervous." She wanted him to go away and to never have to deal with another police officer.

"That's why we need to go over it. Just a few minutes." He smiled, and his handsome face won her over. She was partial to men in dark turtlenecks and knit caps too.

Riley slid the bolt lock and stepped back.

The detective strode inside, his running shoes making a squeaky sound. "Let's sit at the table."

They moved into the kitchen. "Would you like something to drink?" Riley offered.

"You got any Dr. Pepper?"

"Always." They'd guzzled cans of it out of a vending machine during interrogations and trial prep. Riley pulled out a two-liter bottle. "I don't have cans, but I can pour you a glass."

"Sounds good. Pour yourself one too." He leaned back, his long legs stretched out.

She filled his glass most of the way, then poured herself a half portion. It was too late at night for much caffeine. She set the drinks on the table and sat down. "What's the new evidence?"

"It relates to Yano's stolen cars."

"I've told you. I don't know anything about that."

"Did you ever hear him mention a partner?"

"Maybe." The conversation she'd listened to outside Yano's office came back to her. "I overheard him say something to Luke about not having to get into his business with some other guy. But I don't remember the name."

"You're sure?"

"For now. But it might come back to me."

"I could use some ice." Becker held up his glass.

Riley got up. "Sorry. I don't like ice so I forget." She took his drink to the counter and opened the fridge. "I never really suspected anything about Yano's scams. I did notice that all three of his stepdaughters had been in car accidents, which I thought was strange. But then I thought"—she pivoted to the table—"they were just bad drivers."

Becker yanked his hand back from over her soda.

What was that? Had he just roofied her drink? That seemed like crazy thinking. She started to ask him, but the partner name Yano had mentioned popped into her head. *Scott.* She'd heard him mention his stepbrother Scott another time too. Detective Becker's first name was Scott.

Terror filled her body, closing off her throat. Becker was Yano's partner and he was here to kill her before she could testify.

The detective stood, blocking her path to the front door.

Tuck started barking and Riley bolted for the bedroom.

Footsteps pounded down the hall behind her.

She darted through the open door, slammed it behind her, and turned the lock. On the other side, Becker kicked the door, causing it to rattle. Riley stumbled backward. She caught herself and lunged toward the closet where she kept a bat for protection.

Her pulse raced and Tuck barked wildly as she shoved aside dresses and searched the back corners with her hands. *Where the hell was it?*

Another slam into the door, then she heard it open.

Her fingers made contact with the smooth metal. She grabbed it and spun around. Becker's dark frame charged straight at her. Riley pulled back for a swing at his head, but her hands weren't positioned correctly and she only made weak contact with his shoulder. He knocked the bat out of her hands, then slammed his palms into her chest, shoving her with a powerful blow. The wind knocked from her lungs, she gasped for air as she fell back onto the bed.

Becker climbed on top, straddling her.

NoNoNo!

Tuck's bark turned into growls.

Riley struggled but his weight had her pinned. She swung wildly with her fists, but the blows didn't faze him. He reached for a pillow and shoved it into her face, pressing down.

Oh god. She gasped for air and kicked her feet, but she knew she was about to die.

"Auggh!" Her assailant suddenly cried out in pain, then twisted away, loosening his grip.

As he fought to free his ankle from Tuck's teeth, Riley managed to yank the pillow off her face. She tried to scream, but didn't have enough air. She gulped deep breaths and bucked her hips trying to dislodge Becker. Already in a precarious twisted position, with a dog latched onto his ankle, Becker gave up his straddle and planted his feet on the floor. As he kicked wildly, trying to shake Tuck loose, Riley rolled away.

On her feet now, she ran for the bat, lying near the bathroom door.

A thud sounded behind her, followed by a whimper. Rage engulfed her and she grabbed the bat, getting her hands on the grip tape. She spun, weapon at the ready.

Becker came at her again and she swung for his knees this time, making solid contact.

"Bitch!" He lunged and she saw the glint of a knife. Riley swung the bat again, a direct hit to the side of his head.

He was already falling toward her and the knife sliced into her thigh as he collapsed near her feet.

The pain was intense, but adrenaline overpowered it. Riley swung the bat again, smashing it into the back of his head.

Her assailant lay still.

She jumped over him and ran to Tuck. Doggo was on the floor near the dresser, bleeding from one eye. He struggled to his feet as she neared. Riley picked him up. *Please be okay. Please be okay.* Tuck had saved her life. She spun back, but Becker hadn't moved.

Her mind whirled with indecision. Run out of the house? Call the police? Where was her phone?

But she couldn't make herself do any of it. A detective was unconscious, maybe dead, in her house, and she was already branded a criminal. No one would believe her.

Fuck!

The instinct to flee overrode everything else. With Tuck still in her arms, she ran to the bathroom, where she searched for the superglue she used to repair broken heels. She found it in a drawer, then set Tuck on the counter. Pressing the cut on her leg closed with one hand, she squeezed glue with the other, dripping it along the bloody gash. She held the knife wound closed for a count of ten, then dug out an ace bandage and wrapped it tightly around her leg. She tried to bandage Tuck's eye but he wouldn't let her, so she tied a bandana over it and begged him to hold still.

Riley stuck her head back into the bedroom, where Becker lay still, but he was making a soft moaning sound. She grabbed an overnight bag from her closet and stuffed it with clothes, not caring what she packed. Her only thought was to get out and never look back.

Tuck needed help, so she drove to a 24-hour veterinary hospital, where they removed his injured eye and patched him up. The surgery took hours and they wanted to keep him for observation. But she couldn't risk hanging out. Becker wasn't dead, and he knew they were both wounded. He might call or search for late-night medical services.

Around midnight, she carried her sleepy boy to the car and drove south on the freeway until she couldn't keep her eyes open. Riley stopped at a rest area, parked between two big trucks, and slept until daylight.

When she reached Vancouver the next morning, she found a branch of her bank, waited for it to open, then went inside and emptied her account. The teller tried to talk her into taking a cashier's check, but Riley insisted on cash. With Copeland's money from the diamond and another ten thousand in equity from the house, she walked out of the bank with thirty grand tucked into a large, zippered makeup bag. Riley made another stop to buy food for Tuck, then got back on the road. Her goal was to drive through Oregon and reach northern California before nightfall, thinking Redding might be a nice place to relocate.

An hour later, as she pulled off for gas in Wilsonville, her phone rang. *Her mother!* Riley almost didn't answer. It had been years since they'd spoken. But once she went dark, they might never see each other again. Riley took the call. "Hey, Mom."

"Why aren't you in court?" Her mother was angry and shrill.

Like a knife in her chest. Of course that was why she'd called. "I have to protect myself. So you may not hear from me for a long time."

"Riley, no. That's not—"

"Have a nice life." She ended the call, wishing she hadn't bothered to take it. *No.* She'd said goodbye and that felt right.

Pulling out of the gas station, she turned in the wrong direction and ended up driving through Wilsonville. The signs—Coffee Lake Wetlands and Boonsferry Road—made her smile. And the name, Wilsonville, reminded her of Margaritaville, her dad's favorite song and the truth of her current situation: her "own damn fault." She pulled into a park and looked around. Lush, green, and peaceful. Why not just stay?

Chapter 39

The Turbulent Present
His phone was home even if he wasn't

Sept. 11, Tacoma (day 4 after the kidnapping)

Dallas woke with a sense of urgency and jumped out of bed. *Damn.* It was already after seven. She'd worked late, and Yano had woken her twice with his petty, sociopathic texts. But none of that was relevant. Riley Brockwell had been missing for four days, and if Dallas didn't produce a tangible lead soon, her boss would summon her back to Phoenix. She dressed, grabbed coffee and a bagel from the hotel's breakfast bar, and headed out. She would check her email and squeeze in some cardio later. She wanted to catch Copeland before he went anywhere for the day.

His home, a modest but well-kept ranch style, didn't have any lights on. Dallas checked her phone for the time: *8:25.* Too early to call on someone unannounced, but she would do it anyway. Law enforcement didn't run on the same schedule as civilians. The job was around the clock, and she expected Copeland to remember and respect that.

Dallas rang the bell, then pounded on the door in case the old guy couldn't hear high-pitched sounds anymore.

No response.

She pounded again. "Copeland! It's Agent Dallas, FBI. I need your help."

The house stayed silent. He obviously wasn't home. She pulled out her phone and called him, hoping to learn if he was having breakfast somewhere nearby or vacationing in Tahiti. As she listened to the rings, Dallas became aware of an echo, a second trilling sound from inside the house. Copeland's phone was home even if he wasn't. *Odd.*

Maybe he was just a sound sleeper. *Ha!* He was an ex-cop. Even if he drank heavily, he would still be on his feet at the sound of someone pounding on his door. Dallas decided to walk around the block a few times, calling him relentlessly until he answered. She hurried across the stone path to the driveway, then impulsively peeked in the narrow horizontal window of the garage door. A Ford Tahoe sat in the middle, surrounded by tools and outdoor equipment.

Jittery sensations rolled up her spine. His vehicle was here and his phone was here. Unless Copeland had been picked up by an Uber driver on his way to the airport for a phoneless vacation…

Dallas hustled to the front door and pounded again, then grabbed the knob and twisted. The door pushed open. Now her nerves were jumping. Cops didn't leave their homes unlocked. She jogged to her car parked on the street, pulled her weapon from under the seat, and cautiously entered the home.

The place looked ransacked and a man lay face down on the floor in the dining room, his blood drying in the space around him.

Oh shit. Dallas hurried over, knowing he was dead from the gunshot that had torn clean through. She checked his pulse anyway, glancing over her shoulder as she squatted. His skin was cool and the house was quiet, the killer long gone. Dallas checked his jacket pocket, found a wallet with a driver's license, and called 911.

"What's your emergency?"

"Roger Copeland, a retired police officer, is dead in his home from a gunshot."

"What's your name?"

"Dallas, but I don't have time to chat." She rattled off the address, hung up, then called the Tacoma police department. The phone rang a dozen times before she gave up. She called her boss, but he didn't answer either. Dallas left him a message: "Yano may be on a revenge mission. The detective who led the Tacoma investigation was shot dead in his home last night. Text me the names of everyone on that taskforce, including the woman who initiated the investigation, then got sidelined."

She ended the call and ran to the Kia, upset with herself for not remembering their names. But it had been three years. Still, she wanted to warn them. She pressed 911 again. "Agent Dallas, FBI. Patch me through to your chief."

"I don't have that access, and I doubt he's available."

"Just get somebody with authority on the line. Some of your detectives could be in danger."

After a long pause, a voice recording played. "This is Captain Ortega. Please leave a message."

Oh hell! Dallas hung up and started the car. It would be more efficient to just drive over. As she backed out, she spotted a black truck at the end of the street, pulling over to park. A thirty-something man was behind the wheel. The dude was still tailing her. She drove toward him, then spun her vehicle to block his exit. Glock in hand, Dallas jumped out and shouted, "Get out of the truck! Hands in the air!"

Looking terrified, the man did as instructed. "I don't have a gun," he stammered. "And I'm not here to harm you."

Now that she could see his face clearly, Dallas realized how she knew him. She'd briefly targeted this guy as a way to get inside the family's fraud operation—right before they'd abruptly left Phoenix. "JT. I thought you were in prison."

"Early release."

"Why are you following me"

"I'm looking for Riley, and I'm afraid my uncle has her." His voice cracked. "You seemed to be searching for her, so I tagged along."

He sounded sincere, but he'd once been part of the fraud crew, and Riley's testimony had put him away. "What's your interest in Riley?"

"I love her. I always have. Then she disappeared."

That caught her by surprise. "You're a couple?"

He hesitated as a neighborhood car rolled up, squeezed by Dallas' Kia, then honked in irritation.

"Yeah, we've been dating."

Something about this didn't make sense, especially considering what she'd read about Remi/Riley's memory issues. But she didn't have time to get into it. "If you really want to help, tell me where Yano is."

"If I knew I wouldn't be following you." JT stared down at his hands. "My uncle always gets revenge." He looked over her shoulder at Copeland's house. "What happened in there?"

"A murdered detective." But he might already know that. Maybe she should have him arrested. But that would take time she didn't have. "Get in your truck and stay out of my way."

He started to comply, then turned back. "Is Tuck okay? Riley would want someone to take care of him."

He was worried about the dog? "How should I know?" Dallas stepped toward her vehicle, not turning her back. She didn't quite trust this guy.

JT shrugged. "If you had Riley's phone, you could track him."

A flutter of excitement. "Tuck has a GPS chip?"

"Yeah. And Riley has an app for it on her cell."

How had she missed that? Dallas reached in the Kia and pulled the phone from her shoulder bag. The home screen had fewer than a dozen icons and none looked like a pet tracker. "It's not here."

Walking toward her, JT held out his hand. "It's called SafePet, and I think I can find it."

Dallas was already searching the app store and clicked on the tracker he'd just named. The software opened, and a map of their region displayed. In the middle was a red dot. The chip was still active and the dog was only fifteen miles away. "Yes!"

JT tried to look over her shoulder, so Dallas stiff-armed him and climbed in the Kia. "Thanks for your help. Now go home."

She slammed her door and enlarged the phone map to see the chip's exact location. A storage business near the intersection of Roosevelt and 44th Street on the east edge of Tacoma, near Waller. She started the engine and sped off. Another vehicle coming at her on the narrow street reminded her to chill. Just because the dog, or its collar, was in that spot didn't mean Riley Brockwell was. Dallas put in her earbuds and called the Tacoma police department again. They still needed to know that other detectives might be targeted. At the corner, Dallas glanced in her rearview mirror. JT was following again. If he interfered in any way, she would have him arrested.

Chapter 40

The Turbulent Present

Watching the door, a finger on the detonator

Around the same time

Riley took long slow breaths, her eyes closed to shut out the harsh metal walls around her. Yano had left her alone in the storage unit, but she knew he was still nearby... with a detonator, ready to set off the bomb when Becker walked in. The two men must have had a falling out. Maybe the detective had been blackmailing Yano or vice versa. She didn't care. They were both murderous criminals.

Her mouth was covered with a strip of duct tape, the only visual indication something was wrong. A decent cop's instinct would be to run over and help her. But not Becker. Still, the bomb was probably powerful enough to take out someone who stood near the door. Riley worked her jaw back and forth, trying to loosen the tape. It didn't naturally stick to skin, and she thought she could get at least one side free. She'd wanted to be able to warn anyone who opened the door.

At one point, Yano had said "cops," plural, so Becker might not come alone, or he could send someone else. She was disturbingly aware that other detectives had worked Yano's case. Riley brought her bound hands to her face even though they were still trapped in the pouch pocket. Through the sweatshirt material, she rubbed and picked at the duct tape. One side soon pulled free, leaving it dangling from her other cheek. She awkwardly pulled on the strip until it fell to the floor.

Now she waited, for what seemed like an hour, every minute an awareness that she was about to die and that this dark boxy room was the last thing she would ever see. As time passed, the sound of nearby traffic escalated, and at one point, she heard voices on the backside of the unit. People blissfully unaware they were within a few feet of being blown to bits.

Finally, footsteps approached and the metal door rolled open. This was it. The last conversation she would ever have.

Becker stood in the opening, staring, a gun in hand. "What's this about, Riley?"

He seemed to be alone. She visualized Yano, or maybe Blake, watching the door, a finger on the detonator. Would they wait for Becker to step inside? Riley was torn. She hated Becker as much as she hated Yano, but—

More footsteps, then someone stood at his side. Becker spun around, seeming shocked to see the dark-haired woman with a stern expression. The other detective's mouth dropped open too and she shouted, "Riley! What the hell?

Oh god, no. Her mother was here. Yano must have called Carie and summoned her. As the original investigator on the case, her mom might even be his real target.

"Stay out!" Riley screamed. "I have a bomb strapped to me!"

Becker stepped back, but her mother stood firm, the color draining from her face. "I'll call the bomb squad."

"No! Yano is watching and he'll set off the detonator." Riley choked back a sob. "Just run!"

"I'm not leaving you." Her mother's eyes darted around, analyzing the situation.

"You can't help me." Still, Riley wanted her to know the truth, and her mother might believe her now. "Becker tried to kill me. That's why I left town. He and Yano were partners in the car-theft business."

Carie spun toward Becker, stunned.

Becker shook his head. "You know me, Silva. Riley's obviously the one working with Yano."

Her mother vacillated, eyes darting between Riley and her fellow officer.

During her talks with Copeland, Riley had learned that her mother had started investigating Yano's crew a year before the accident. Her cop instinct about him had been right from the start. Once Riley had become involved in the crimes, Detective Carie Silva had quietly sidelined herself. She'd also stopped speaking to Riley, except that day she'd called when Riley missed court on her way out of town.

"Riley," her mother prodded, not taking her eyes off Becker. "How am I supposed to believe you? Give me something solid."

Riley's head spun. What did she know that would be convincing? Then it came to her, the way it had when Becker had been at her place. "I overheard Yano say his partner was his step-brother Scott. When I told Becker that, he attacked me."

Her mother pulled her weapon, aiming at Becker's midsection. "You son-of-a-bitch!"

Becker raised his gun too. "Drop it, Silva. You're making a mistake."

A heavy moment of silence.

Then two loud shots blasted outside the storage space, shattering the quiet.

Chapter 41

The Turbulent Present
A hit man, a thrill seeker, or stupidly in love

Ten minutes earlier

As she drove south, Dallas vacillated about whether to call 911 again. She'd already reported Copeland's death, and knowing how police departments responded, at least five patrol cars were on their way to his house. The retired detective had been killed the night before, so Yano could be anywhere, and most of those officers would be wasting their time. She hated to sideline even more units off their regular patrols for what could turn out to be nothing more than a dog, or just a collar, picked up by a traveler and transported north.

To a location within fifteen miles of Copeland's murder?

She pressed the emergency numbers and waited through six rings and their standard greeting.

"Agent Dallas again. I need backup at the storage place near the intersection of Roosevelt and Forty-Fourth."

"Backup for what?" A male dispatcher this time, who sounded impatient.

"I'm not sure yet." *How to explain this?* "A dog with a tracking chip, who belongs to a missing woman, is showing in that spot."

"Is the missing woman a current Tacoma police investigation?"

Dallas let loose with sarcasm and seniority. "She's a concern for the Federal Bureau of Investigation, but your people are closer than mine."

"I'll send a unit."

"Thanks." Dallas pressed her earbud and braked for the turn onto Roosevelt. A quick glance back to see if JT was still hanging on. Yes, indeed. He was either a hit man, a thrill seeker, or stupidly in love with Riley Brockwell.

At the next traffic light, she checked the SafePet map again. The red dot hadn't moved. What if the signal was just a digital glitch? She would know soon enough. She sat at the intersection, scanning sidewalks, cars, and businesses. Not only was she looking for a Jack Russell terrier, but also a woman matching Riley's description. And possibly a man matching Yano's. But the grifter hadn't been seen in public for years, so he could be grayer and fatter. Or bald and shriveled now. She also had no idea what he was driving.

The car behind her honked, so she looked up to see the green light and rolled through the intersection. Her phone beeped in her earbud and she took the call.

"It's Radner."

"What have you got?"

"The names you needed. Carie Silva and Scott Becker were the other detectives on the taskforce. Saul Wheeler from our Seattle bureau also joined them, but he was transferred to DC last year."

"Thanks." Dallas vaguely remembered Becker now, a good-looking man, but she'd never met Silva, only read her reports.

"What's the update on Copeland's death?" Radner asked. "Are you searching his place?"

"Tacoma police are handling it. I'm tracking a new lead."

"Do you need backup?"

"It's on the way." Still scanning, she spotted a tall man in black jeans and charcoal-gray jacket at a gas station. The clothes and posture made her think law enforcement. "Hey, do you have descriptions of Becker and Silva? I know I worked with Becker, but it was three years ago and only for a week. And Silva left the team right before I started consulting.

"Let me see what I can find."

"Better yet, call the Tacoma police department and warn them of the danger." Dallas was sure she'd remember Becker if she saw him. The tall guy she'd just spotted wasn't familiar, except his basic vibe.

"What specific danger?" Radner was clearly concerned.

"Just that Yano might be in revenge mode with nothing to lose. I have to go." She ended the call before he could tell her to hold off until she had backup.

Dallas checked the pet app again, enlarging the map until the dot showed clearly in a parking area about a half mile away. But GPS maps could sometimes be off by an even greater distance. The satellites recording and sending the information were hundreds of miles above the earth.

She passed a park with a large pond, where swans floated by. Dallas turned onto 44th, and the landscape morphed into rural plots, many undeveloped. Near the next intersection, she slowed, passing a miniature golf course that didn't look open. Beyond it, a huge storage business spanned both sides of the corner with a mobile home park across the road.

Dallas pulled into the narrow space in front of Pioneer Storage. A ten-foot, chain-link fence surrounded the property, with the units accessible through a rolling gate that required a security code. She checked the phone map again. If the locator was accurate, the red dot was in the back of this property. Or possibly behind the miniature golf course. Dallas jogged into the front office, where an older couple were arguing about cutting the lock off a unit. They barely glanced at her, so she loudly announced herself. "Agent Dallas, FBI. I need access to units in the back."

The man looked her over, with a head dip she'd seen hundreds of times. "You're better lookin' than the detectives who just went back there."

Oh hell. "A man and a woman?"

"Yeah."

"What unit?"

"Eighty-six, in the back corner." He pointed to the miniature golf side.

The wife, who'd been glaring at her husband, turned to Dallas. "What's goin' on?"

"Just give me the code."

"Five-nine-five-zero, but like I told the others, we can't let you into a unit without a warrant."

"I probably won't need this, but just in case." She grabbed the massive bolt cutters on the counter.

"Hey! You can't take that." The old guy started around the end of the counter.

Dallas rushed to her Kia, locked the doors in case the storage owner got aggressive, and rolled up to the security post. As she punched in the code, the old guy knocked on her window. She ignored him while the gate opened, then eased through. She might be wrong about the dog-collar chip, but a cop was dead and others might be walking into a trap. She had probable cause.

The narrow space between the metal buildings and the fence forced her to drive slowly. She also had to check the east-west rows of the grid as she passed. The one car she saw was a lime-green Volkswagen bug. Not Yano's style, even if he was trying to hide in plain sight.

She spotted two dark sedans near the end of the row. The detectives.

Beyond them, the perimeter looked odd. Dallas eased forward, realizing that someone had cut out a section of the fence. The opening was big enough for a vehicle to pass through. On the other side was a gravel lot behind the golf course.

Something sketchy was happening here. She cut her engine, coasted to a stop, and got out. She grabbed her Glock and stayed low, moving toward the sedans. As she scooted forward, she scanned the golf course on the right and occasionally glanced at the storage units… in case one opened.

As she crept past the first sedan, she finally saw two people in dark blazers standing in the doorway of the last unit on the end. Becker was a few feet outside the space, and the woman, Silva, was just inside.

Dallas heard a noise and pivoted to the golf course. An oversized bald guy lunged from behind a fake rock in the back corner. In one hand, he held a gun with a silencer, and in the other he seemed to have a small remote-like device. Both were aimed at the detectives.

Dallas reacted instinctively, raising her Glock to take two shots. The big guy went down and both detectives spun toward her. Before she could call out her FBI status, an engine roared in the lot behind the golf course. Dallas ran toward the hole in the fence and scurried through. As the 4Runner spun in the gravel, she identified Yano in the passenger seat. A moment later, the vehicle sped away.

She ran back toward the storage place where her car was parked and realized the two officers had guns drawn on each other.

What the hell?

Dallas stopped short, her own weapon still in her hand. "What's going on? Backup is on the way." She focused on Silva, hoping the woman could be trusted.

"My daughter has a bomb strapped to her chest."

Holy shit!

Chapter 42

The Turbulent Present
The need burned like an ulcer in his gut

A few minutes earlier

Oh fuck! Blake was down and the bomb hadn't gone off. "Go!" Yano shouted.

"What? We can't just leave him." Seth's face filled with panic and he reached for his door handle.

"We have to!" The dipshit didn't understand. "Becker and Silva aren't dead yet, so they're calling in more cops."

Seth scowled, pressed the accelerator, and spun the 4Runner around. They sped across the parking area, tires spinning, throwing gravel. Seth careened around the back corner of the golf course and raced out the side driveway. "Where to?"

"The ferry, just like I planned." Yano slammed the dashboard. "Damn! I wanted them blown to pieces." People who fucked him over had to pay. He'd always felt that way, but now that his days were numbered, the need burned like an ulcer in his gut.

"But Riley, she's still gonna blow, right?"

Yano checked the timer he'd set on his phone to match the timer on the bomb. "She's only got seven minutes left, and the bomb squad obviously ain't here yet." Yano gestured at the storage place. No squad cars, no fire trucks, no armored units.

"But they're comin'." At the road, Seth turned right and gunned the engine. "What do ya think happened? With Blake, I mean."

"Scott musta shot him. That shifty prick has been shakin' me down since our operation went south." He and Scott had grown up together and stayed close, but once the cash flow ran dry, even his stepbrother had turned on him. Yano slammed his palm twice more. "Now all those haters will get away with what they did to me. I don't have time to do this setup again."

"Yeah, sorry about that." Seth shot him a look of pity.

Yano punched his arm. "Don't fuckin' do that. I'm going out my own way. How many people have the balls to pull that off?"

"Damn few." Seth shook his head. "My mother died in a nursing home in a pile of her own shit. I'd rather take a bullet like Blake did."

Yano laughed. "I'm gonna die on a beach in Mexico, soaking up sun and jerking off."

"How long have you got?"

Yano wasn't sure. He'd stopped seeing the cancer doctor long ago. "As long as I get to pound Donna a few more times, I'm good." He kept telling himself that, but it was bullshit. He felt ripped off in so many ways. And his run of bad luck had all started with Riley not having the good sense to just stay on the road. She'd plowed his son into a tree, killing poor Luke, then spilled her guts to the cops like a traitor. He'd pleaded with her, using Luke as emotional leverage, but she'd hung up on him. The day before his wife went to trial, he'd sent Matt to bribe Riley, and if that didn't work, to demand his beautiful ring back. The bitch had told him to fuck off. That was the moment he'd decided to kill her rather than let her testify against him. His shifty stepbrother had easily taken the bait. All he'd had to do was insinuate to Scott that Riley knew about his involvement with the stolen cars. But somehow, the bitch had evaded her well-deserved fate.

Riley was like a black cloud hanging over him, and the stress of her betrayal had given him cancer. The little bitch had never once mentioned her mother was a cop! If he'd known, he would've never let Luke marry her. Scott had failed him on that front too, claiming Silva never talked about her family so he hadn't known. Yano had wanted to beat him down for that. But his stepbrother was bigger… and a dirty cop… who'd failed to sabotage the investigation into him.

"Almost there." Seth grinned.

Yano nodded. His driver was a loose end too, but with Blake dead, Seth would probably just get the hell out of town. Yano's thoughts came back to Riley, as they always did. Getting blown to bits was too good for her, too easy. But the idea of taking out most of his enemies with one bomb had seemed perfect. Splashy, satisfying, and efficient. But Scott had fucked him over again and now his time was running out.

Yano glanced over his shoulder at the dog, still caged in the back seat. He didn't need the mutt for leverage anymore, but he kinda liked the little turd and didn't particularly want to hurt him. Still, the dog had to go. How to get rid of a caged critter without dropping him in public where someone would notice?

Sirens in the distance made Yano's skin crawl. But those cops were racing to the storage place, so he should be in the clear for a while. Once the bomb went off in a few minutes, there would be no one to connect him to the scene, and nobody knew what he was driving or where he was headed. He just had to reach the Point Defiance ferry terminal, cross the water to Vashon Island, then drive a few miles to an airfield. After lifting off on a private charter flight, he'd be on his way to Mexico to live out his final days with Donna.

Once he was gone, she would still have a sweet bank account, thanks to the stock tips Riley had picked up. A small payback for all she'd cost him—his son, his home, his lifestyle, and nearly his freedom too. Yano checked his phone timer and smiled. The bitch would soon be dead.

Chapter 43

The Turbulent Present
Or the timer would run down

A few minutes earlier

Riley didn't know who had fired the shot or if anyone had been hurt, but a blonde woman with a big silver gun approached the storage unit. She was either law enforcement or an assassin. Becker and her mother glanced at the newcomer without taking their eyes or weapons off each other.

"What's going on? Backup is coming." The woman focused on her mother.

"My daughter has a bomb strapped to her chest."

"Oh hell." The woman moved closer, peered into the storage space at Riley, then turned back to Carie. "Agent Dallas, FBI."

Her mom waved her gun at Becker again. "Drop your weapon." She glanced over at the agent. "This dirty cop already tried to kill Riley once."

Becker eased sideways, away from the women. "If you move on me, I'll shoot you both."

Riley could only watch, terrified for all of them. The bomb was still set to go off.

Her mother fired, the sound deafening.

Becker doubled over, bleeding from his belly. He tried to raise his weapon, but dropped to the ground instead.

The agent swore, wide-eyed.

"I got this," her mother yelled. "A bomb squad is on the way. Go after Yano!"

The blonde woman hesitated for a second, then turned and ran.

Carie hurried over to Becker, took his weapon, and cuffed him. Leaving him bleeding, she moved toward the unit's opening.

"Get out of here," Riley begged. "I've hurt enough people."

Her mom shook her head, tears welling in her eyes. "It wasn't your fault. I'm sorry for judging you so harshly and pushing you out of my life."

Taken aback, Riley cherished the words as they washed over the deep wounds in her soul. "I'm sorry for causing you so much pain and humiliation."

"I love you, Riley."

Why had her mother waited until this moment to say it? When it was too late to matter?

Was it too late? The timer was simply an app on the phone. Maybe the only thing preventing her from defusing the bomb was her bound hands. "Can you cut my ties? Please. I think I can stop this." Despite all she'd lost, Riley wanted to live.

Blinking rapidly, her mom stepped tentatively into the storage space. "What ties? Your hands?"

"My wrists are zip-tied inside the pouch."

"We should wait for the bomb squad."

"We don't have time!" It seemed like hours had passed already.

Her mother looked around frantically. "Is there a knife or something sharp in here?"

She had nail scissors! "In my right pocket," Riley said. "In the shorts under the sweatpants."

As her mother rushed forward, Riley arched her hips off the chair. Carie pulled down the sweats, then shoved her fingers into the tight pocket and fished out the tiny scissors.

"Oh my god." Mumbling to herself, her mom cut through the cloth pouch, exposing Riley's hands, then snipped the plastic ties.

"Now go!" Riley yelled. "But leave me the scissors."

Her mother kissed her forehead and hurried out, not stopping until she was ten feet beyond the opening.

Riley took a deep breath. Based on everything she'd seen Yano do and say, the essence of the bomb's trigger was the phone. Either it would ring and go off—which hadn't happened—or the timer would run down, setting off the detonator. Staring at all the wiring had been pointless. She just needed to stop the timer, and there was no harm in trying.

Riley yanked off her sweatshirt, then gently pulled the device from its sleeve next to the explosive sticks. The old iPhone was still attached to the middle tube with about seven inches of wire and its screen was dark. Hands shaking, Riley pressed the Home button. The screen illuminated, but nothing showed, no timer, no icons. Cursing, she gently swiped left. A few icons appeared, with Clock in the middle. Again, she held her breath as she pressed the screen. The app opened, filling the space with its timer software and a countdown flashing: 2:05, 2:04, 2:03.

Was it really this simple?

Maybe she should cut the white wire. *No.* It could trigger the detonator.

Riley stared at the two circles under the flashing numbers.

One said Cancel, and the other Pause. Both should work. What did she have to lose?

She pressed Cancel.

The numbers stopped, then disappeared.

Tension drained from her body—but this wasn't over yet. She still had explosives on her chest, and a detonator phone was out there somewhere. Riley delicately lifted the vest off her shoulders, then over her head. She set it gently on the floor, then bolted out of the storage unit.

Her mother's arms opened wide and Riley fell into them, sobbing with relief.

Chapter 44

The Turbulent Present

Worst-case scenarios flashed in her mind

Around the same time

With her phone in her lap, Dallas followed the moving dot on the map, zig-zagging north and west. Her best assessment: Yano was headed to an ocean port. Or maybe just to a coastal route out of the state, one that wasn't patrolled by troopers. Canada was only a few hours away.

She pressed her earbud. "Call 911."

A female dispatcher this time. "What's your emergency?"

"Agent Dallas, FBI. I'm following a murder suspect and need backup."

"What's your location?"

She wasn't sure. "I'm heading northwest away from Pioneer Storage."

"The bomb threat site?" Surprise in the dispatcher's tone.

"Yes. I'm following Aden Sebastiano, aka Yano. He's in the passenger seat of a dark-gray 4Runner."

"This may take a few minutes. We just sent all available patrols to the storage site."

"The bomber is on the move and I need help. I'll keep you

posted on my location." Dallas ended the call, then realized she should have left the line open. But she couldn't drive and follow the GPS locator and answer questions at the same time.

The car ahead suddenly slowed and she had to slam her brakes. The red dot shifted again, and Dallas turned onto Sixth Avenue, heading west. She had to assume the dog was still in the 4Runner with Yano. The fact that the red dot was still on the move gave her confidence. It was possible Yano had tossed the collar into a vehicle going another direction, but she had no reason to think he'd suddenly discovered the chip. Although at some point, she expected him to abandon the dog... unless keeping Riley's pet was part of his demented revenge plot.

Dallas passed a Sonic burger place, grimaced that she'd missed another meal, then noticed a cannabis store next door. Good sense business grouping. The red dot abruptly turned right onto Pearl, so she did too. The road soon widened into Highway 63, heading straight north. Based on the micro-map her phone produced, Yano would soon run out of road as the Tacoma geography came to a point that stuck out into the Puget Sound.

What the hell? She wasn't personally familiar with the Sea-Tac water-centric metropolis, except what she'd studied briefly in her hotel room, so she'd run out of guesses for Yano's next move. He and his family of grifters had lived in the area for the past six years, so he'd had time to learn all the suburbs, islands, and waterways.

Ten minutes later, a road sign spelled it out: *Point Defiance Ferry Terminal.*

He was headed to an island in the sound. That seemed like a surprisingly dead-end choice. Unless he planned to cross the island and take another ferry. All of that seemed slow and cumbersome for someone on the run. But the route wouldn't be obvious or heavily patrolled by law enforcement. At this point, she was the only officer with any direct knowledge of his location, and he probably didn't know she was back here.

She pressed her earbud to re-dial and got the male dispatcher she'd talked to earlier. "Agent Dallas again. The bomb suspect, Aden Sebastiano, is headed toward the Point Defiance Ferry. Where does it go?"

A pause. "Vashon Island."

"Have the Vashon police meet the next ferry. As far as I know, Yano is still driving a 4Runner."

"They only have two officers, but I'll make the request."

"Thanks." Dallas started to click off, then asked, "Is there another ferry off the island?"

"I think so." A pause. "There's also a small airfield."

Oh hell. Now the route made sense. "Put the airport on alert for Yano too."

Chapter 45

The Turbulent Present
This could go sideways in five directions

Ten minutes later

Dallas sat in a double line of cars, waiting on a downhill slope to board the ferry. The view was amazing: blue sky over shimmering water with a mountain peak in the background. In this moment, she didn't care. Being boxed in was driving her crazy. She wanted to get out and run ahead to be sure the 4Runner was near the front of the line with Yano in it. It was impossible to tell from back here, behind a dozen other vehicles. Yet she hated to leave her car, in case Yano wasn't in the line, or he saw her approaching and sped off, leaving her on foot.

She also wanted to arrest him ASAP, but didn't want to risk confronting him and his driver without backup. They were both likely armed. The man she'd shot outside the storage unit had been, and the whole crew was clearly determined to kill police officers. Worst-case scenarios flashed in her mind. The Vashon police wouldn't show, or Yano would somehow switch vehicles on the ferry, then get away. Or maybe the island police would be waiting, then get gunned down as Yano sped by.

The car ahead moved forward, so Dallas let her foot off the

brake. The stop-and-start continued for another five minutes while she played out possibilities in her head. As she neared the ferry's boarding ramp, the two lanes merged into one, and a narrow admin building came into view. A toll booth jutted out on the left. Should she notify the toll-taker of her armed-federal-agent status? This whole scenario with a car-carrying boat was new to her. Phoenix was landlocked and dry.

With only two vehicles still ahead of her, a bell clanged and a railroad-style gate came down, blocking access. *Shit!* The cargo bay was full. Dallas shut off her engine, her brain scrambling. She tucked her Glock into the back of her pants and dug in her shoulder bag for handcuffs. What else would she need? Her badge and phone were still in her blazer pockets. She climbed out, ran to the booth, and showed the old guy her badge.

"I'm following a killer." She handed him her key fob. "If you don't hear back from me, call the bureau."

"You can't just leave your car!"

Dallas ducked under the gate and jogged toward the dark bay filled with three lanes of vehicles. Behind her, a male voice called out, "I'm with her."

She glanced back to see JT still following her. *What the fuck?* She wanted to yell at him, but wouldn't risk drawing attention to herself. Nor did she have time to deal with him—unless he got in her way.

Keeping to the side of the cold steel wall, she searched for the gray 4Runner. In the dim light, it was hard to distinguish one gray crossover SUV from another. Announcements she couldn't understand came over a loudspeaker, then a whistle blew and the ferry started to move.

A moment later, JT caught up to her and whispered, "Do you see Yano? And Riley?"

He didn't know about the bomb. "Riley's not with him, so please stay out of my way."

JT blinked rapidly. "Where is she?"

"Back at the storage unit. Now shut up and let me work." Dallas eased forward, scanning the boat's midsection.

JT grabbed her arm. "Is she okay? What about Tuck?"

"I don't know!" Dallas yanked free. "I will cuff you to that grip bar if you don't back off." Staying low, she scurried to the front, but didn't see the 4Runner. *Damn.* Not willing to risk being seen, Dallas jogged to the back of the ferry, glancing at drivers, in case Yano and his thug had somehow switched vehicles. A few passengers exited their cars and headed for the upper deck to enjoy a more-scenic cruise.

She doubted Yano would join them. Dallas crossed the ferry's back end and started up the other side. Halfway, she spotted the 4Runner just as the driver climbed out. She didn't recognize the skinny man from any of the file photos. That didn't surprise her. Yano's insurance-fraud crew had been mostly family and friends. A few had gone to prison, and others had probably cut ties with their sociopathic patriarch. Yano's new thugs were obviously a more-criminal sort. She wondered what the grifter had been up to these past few years. His type never quit scamming. Even in prison, they found ways to con others out of their canteen money or cigarettes.

She watched the driver as he headed for the stairs. He had hollow cheeks and scraggly hair like a meth addict and kept his head down, as though avoiding security cameras. His hands were in his jacket pockets, and his gait a little heavy on the right side, like someone carrying a gun.

Was this her opportunity to arrest Yano? Cuff him and shove him into—

No. Just watch and wait until she had backup.

What if the island police didn't show, or were late? Her targets were in a vehicle and she was on foot. She couldn't let their SUV exit the ferry. The airport was only a five-minute drive, and once they were in the air, tracking and apprehending them would be significantly more challenging. Dallas dropped to a squat and duck-walked to the back of the 4Runner. Using her thumbnail, she pressed the valve stem of the outside tire and let out the air.

Footsteps on the stairs startled her. The methhead driver was returning, probably from a quick trip to the bathroom. Dallas scurried between two cars, staying low.

A man rolled down his window and grinned at her. "What ya doin'?"

"Shhh. Tracking a criminal." Apprehension squeezed Dallas' chest. This could go sideways in five directions. Too many bystanders.

She glanced back at Yano's vehicle. JT had walked up to it and was peering in the back window. *The idiot!*

Methhead strode up behind him, grabbed JT by the neck, and slammed his head into the plexiglass. Then he pulled a handgun from inside his jacket and pressed it against the back of JT's head.

Oh shit! Dallas sprang to her feet, reaching for her Glock. "FBI! Hands in the air!"

Methhead pivoted toward her, his weapon aimed at her chest.

She fired twice. The twin blasts were deafening, amplified by the metal container.

Yano's driver staggered back, falling against the 4Runner. In a nearby car, a woman started screaming.

As Dallas lunged toward the men, Methhead collapsed to the ground. She squatted, yanked his weapon, and stuffed it into her back waistband. She considered cuffing him, but he was bleeding profusely from holes in his neck and chest, and she only had one set of cuffs.

She heard the 4Runner's passenger door open, so she pushed upright. Yano was running toward the stairs, carrying a dog against his chest. *The prick!* Dallas sprinted after him, and so did JT. She stiff-armed her stalker at the base of the steps. "Stay back!"

Pounding up the stairs, she tried to predict Yano's next move. Unless he went into the water, he was trapped. She feared he would take a hostage. Dallas burst onto the deck, just as Yano reached the railing. Two teenage girls stood nearby. They looked up from their phones to smile at the older man in a tracksuit with a cute pet. More passengers were farther down the deck.

Yano bellowed, "Stay back or I'll kill the dog!"

Dallas didn't see a gun. Or a knife. She walked toward him, her Glock pointed at his head. "Hands in the air!"

In one quick move, Yano flung the terrier over the railing and grabbed one of the girls, pulling her in front of his body.

Her friend screamed, and the hostage girl fainted. The weight of her unconscious body made her drop out of Yano's grip.

Still moving toward him, Dallas yelled, "Hands up!"

Yano suddenly charged her.

Not wanting to risk a shot with young girls behind him, she stepped to the side and throat-punched Yano as he reached her.

"Ugghh!" He reached for his throat, gasping and making choking sounds.

Dallas snap-kicked him in the groin, and he sank to his knees. As she cuffed Yano's hands behind his back, she became aware that passengers were shouting in distress.

One yelled, "Dog overboard!"

She looked up to see JT running past and yanking off his jacket. At the railing, he took off his sneakers.

What the hell?

The idiot went into the water, presumably to save the dog. Dallas hoped they both knew how to swim. Her part in stopping Yano's crime spree was over.

Chapter 46

The Not So Turbulent Present
You saved me from a life I hated

An hour later

Riley leaned back against the couch and closed her eyes. She just wanted to sleep, then wake up in her own bed.

"Let's take a break." Agent Wheeler leaned forward in his chair. "Want some coffee?" The slim, silver-haired man had been soft-spoken, but relentless with his questions. He was the only taskforce investigator left. She'd just learned that her friend Copeland was dead and Becker had been arrested. Her mother was in the room, but only as support.

Riley shook her head. "I'd love a Dr. Pepper."

"Sorry. I don't think the machine has any."

"I have one in my office." Her mom, sitting next to her, stood. "I'll be right back."

They were in the *soft* interview room at the Tacoma Police Department and being here was giving Riley *deja vu*. Years earlier, she'd spent most of a day on this couch, answering questions from Detectives Copeland and Becker. Like then, today's conversation was all about Yano. After this, she never wanted to hear his name again. He'd ruined her life twice. Riley started to cry.

Agent Wheeler looked uncomfortable, his blue eyes darting around. "A few more questions, then we'll call it a day."

Riley sat up and wiped her tears. She'd already told the whole story of her kidnapping and the crazy stuff they'd made her do. Now she just wanted to get this over with so she could go home. Whatever that meant. Wilsonville was hours away, and without Tuck, would never be the same.

Her mother came back with a can of soda. "It's not very cold."

"I don't care." Riley took it, popped the tab, and guzzled a third. "What else do you want to know?"

"Everything Yano said about his wife's current location. And every word Donna Mackey said to you. If she helped plot this—"

A uniformed officer opened the door. "Another FBI agent is here with a witness."

Oh god. Riley couldn't take anymore. "Can it wait? I'm exhausted and I need a shower." They *had* fed her pizza, so she wasn't starving for the first time in days. But despite being stunned and grateful to be alive, she was depressed and sinking into the darkness again. Tuck was gone.

The blonde woman who'd showed up at the storage place stepped into the room. "Agent Dallas." She nodded at the silver-haired man. "Good to see you, Wheeler. I've been worried you were next on the hit list."

"Radner called. It's nice to know you care." He winked at the pretty agent.

Still in the doorway, Dallas grinned at Riley. "I've been tracking you for days. Glad to know you survived this ordeal."

Riley hated to say his name, but she had to know. "What about Yano?"

"I apprehended him on a ferry headed for an island airport." The agent paused. "And shot both of his thugs."

Relief flooded her and Riley had to hold back tears again. The hardest question of all. "What about Tuck?" She regretted asking. Her heart had already assumed he wouldn't survive.

"Crazy thing." Agent Dallas smiled again. "JT, whom I think you know, jumped into the water to save him."

JT? How did he— Riley couldn't think about that confusion right now. Tuck was alive! She pushed off the couch. "Where is he?"

"They're both here and still a little wet."

Dallas moved away from the door, and JT walked in, carrying Tuck.

Riley's heart burst with joy. Tuck wiggled free, yipping and whining as he rushed to her. She scooped him up, hugging him tightly, then sat back on the couch, unable to contain his joyous energy. When doggo finally settled down, she stood and locked eyes with JT. Once her memories had come back, she'd realized he was Thomas, but she'd assumed he was still working with Yano. Thank god she'd been wrong.

"You jumped into the sound? And risked your life to save him. Thank you."

JT silently moved toward her and opened his arms. Riley melted into his embrace. She loved this man, no matter what he called himself.

"We'll clear the room and give you guys a moment," Dallas said. "But there's something I need to know first."

"What?"

"I found a key in your safe in Wilsonville." The pretty agent shrugged. "I broke into it, hoping to help you."

"It's all good. And thank you, by the way. Arriving when you did and shooting Blake saved my life. My mother's too."

"I'm pleased it worked out. I had kind of assumed you were dead, but I wanted to put Yano in prison. We're all better off without him." Dallas cocked her head. "So, is the key for a safe deposit box?"

"Yeah. My birth certificate is in there, along with some paperwork I found in Luke's desk when I moved. I think it incriminates Yano and his family for stuff they did in Phoenix."

"Great news." Dallas high-fived Agent Wheeler. "Maybe we can close our file too. Now let's give these two some space."

When everyone had left, JT hugged her again. "I love you, Riley. I have since that day we all spent at the lake five years ago."

"I love you too, John Thomas." She eased away and picked up Tuck, feeling insecure. "How did you find me?"

"I saw Tuck's picture in the news." He blushed. "After you disappeared from Tacoma, I worried you were dead, but I never gave up. When I got out of prison, I set up a Google alert for both of you." He bent over and petted Tuck's head.

His devotion overwhelmed her, but now their reacquaintance back in August felt strange. "When you saw me at the support group, why didn't you tell me who you were?"

"I wanted to. But the article said you'd lost your memory, and I was afraid that bringing up my connection to Yano might trigger you. I wanted to go slow and see if you remembered me on your own."

She believed him. "I'd like to think I would have."

His eyes clouded. "Do you remember everything now?"

He meant about Luke's death. She didn't want to go there yet. "I'm sorry I testified against you and put you in prison."

"I'm not." He leaned in and kissed her gently. "You saved me from a life I hated. Yano had all of us in his debt, a soul-crushing grip on everyone connected to him. I might have never gotten out."

They both knew the real cost of their freedom had been Luke's life. Could they live with that? "We'll need some therapy." Riley let out a small laugh and felt herself smiling. "Tuck too. He's been traumatized. But I have a counselor who's sort of in the loop already."

JT laughed too. "Maybe she'll give us a family discount."

Thanks for buying and reading my work!

If you liked the story, please visit my website where I offer a free ebook just for joining my mailing list. If you've already read the story offered, contact me for another one. Be reassured, I only send notifications for new releases and occasional discounts on books. If you continue to enjoy my work, please leave ratings or reviews online. Your support helps me keep writing.

https://www.ljsellers.com

If you have an extra moment, follow me on BookBub for new release alerts!

https://www.bookbub.com/authors/l-j-sellers

Here's a complete list of my work.

Detective Jackson Mysteries:
    The Sex Club
    Secrets to Die For
    Thrilled to Death
    Passions of the Dead
    Dying for Justice
    Liars, Cheaters & Thieves
    Rules of Crime
    Crimes of Memory
    Deadly Bonds
    Wrongful Death
    Death Deserved
    A Bitter Dying

A Liar's Death
A Crime of Hate
The Black Pill
Silence of the Dead

Agent Dallas Thrillers:
The Trigger
The Target
The Trap

Extractor Series:
Guilt Game
Broken Boys
The Other

Standalone Thrillers:
Afterstrike
The Wall
No Consent
The Gender Experiment
Point of Control
The Baby Thief
The Gauntlet Assassin
The Lethal Effect

Interesting things to know about me:

I'm a 5-time winner of the Readers' Favorite Awards, I've performed standup comedy, biked over Donner Pass, jumped out of an airplane, and rescued my grandchildren from a dangerous cult in Costa Rica (much like my character The Extractor).

If you liked Agent Dallas, she's featured in eight books, including several with Detective Jackson, my award-winning series. Here's an excerpt from their latest thriller adventures.

The Black Pill

A Jackson & Dallas Thriller

By L.J. Sellers

Chapter 1

Saturday, September 14, 6:27 a.m.

Bettina Rios pulled on running shoes, grabbed her cell phone from the dresser, and clicked the Strava icon. But she wouldn't start the mileage app yet. First she had to check on her mother. Across the hall, she tapped lightly on the other bedroom door. "Mama? You awake?"

"Si."

Bettina stepped in, braced for the clutter and smell. Her mother loved glass figurines and tacky paintings and had managed to accumulate a substantial collection in the short time they'd been here. The old woman sat in her wheelchair, wearing stained sweatpants and a red sweater with holes in it, her gray hair a mess. She only changed clothes when Bettina helped her shower. Her mother hated the whole undignified process, so they didn't do it often.

"How are you?" Bettina always spoke English to Mama and encouraged her to do the same. The skill might save their lives someday.

"I no sleep." Her weak voice made Bettina's heart hurt. Mama had been so strong, so fearless. But the long journey had taken its toll, and now she couldn't do much of anything.

"Maybe less coffee." Bettina smiled gently, knowing she had wasted her breath. Her mother ate and drank whatever she wanted. That's how she'd ended up in this mess. The stubborn woman was probably diabetic but wouldn't see a doctor or take any help from "strangers." So Bettina did it all. The situation was challenging to work around, so she kept their finances afloat with gig jobs. Her main one was really strange, but paid well.

She kissed Mama's forehead and wheeled her into the kitchen. "Fruit and toast?"

"Just toast. With *mermalada*." A crooked smile eased onto her sun-weathered face. "That counts as fruit."

"Sure." Bettina fixed whatever made her mother happy. Today, that was toast spread thick with strawberry jam. She noticed the fridge was low on cheese and wine, the two things her mother loved most, so she would make a trip to the store later. After handing over the plate, Bettina asked, "What else can I do for you?"

"*Nada*. Later, you can help me write to Ernesto." Bettina's older brother who was still in their home country. Mama waved a crippled blue-veined hand. "Go run. I'll be fine."

Feeling guilty as usual, Bettina headed out, locking the door behind her. On the sidewalk, she pressed the Strava record button and the screen changed to a map. She clicked Start and slid the phone into her fanny pack.

Jogging down the quiet, low-rent street, she squinted in the near darkness. Her eyes would adjust soon, and the sun would rise before she finished her run. She didn't care for the darkness, but in the summer months, she liked to get her workout done before the temperature rose and before she showered and dressed for the day. Using the Strava app was rather silly, because she didn't vary her route much. But she liked keeping track of her miles and being connected to others who were as obsessed with exercise as she was. All of it helped keep her accountable. If she skipped a day, one of her followers would ping her and want to know why. She did the same for them.

A wave of apprehension rolled over her. Would her ex-boyfriend use the app as a way to get to her? What a mistake he'd been. So emotional and possessive. But she'd been lonely for so long, she'd let her guard down and trusted a *chico sexy* who'd smiled at her in that special way. Bettina shook it off, reassuring herself again that using Strava was fine. Aaron didn't exercise and wasn't tech savvy, so he'd never find her that way. The loneliness of her life was nearly unbearable, and the low-key social network gave her some interaction.

At the corner, she turned left on Lombard and headed toward the river park. From there, she would run north on the bike path to the Owosso bridge, cross over, and run back on the other side of the river. The whole loop, including the five blocks to and from her house, covered four and a half miles. She'd hoped to improve her conditioning over time, but the extra weight on her petite body slowed her down.

She'd been running her whole life, one way or another. As a kid, she'd dashed around the beach with her brother, a never-ending game of chase. Years later, when her breasts developed, she'd run from gang members who wanted to rape her and claim her as their property. After they'd caught her, she and Mama had left the first time. Now she jogged to keep her brain from going *loco*—and to burn off all the cheese and chocolate she loved to eat.

Bettina approached the narrow entrance to the park and tensed, wishing for a little more daylight. Overgrown with trees on both sides, the tucked-away access lane was the only part of the route that made her feel vulnerable. She touched the canister of mace she wore around her neck and picked up her pace. As she rounded the turn, she heard something snap. Bettina jerked her head toward the noise. Nothing but eerie shadows under the overhanging trees. Relieved to see the parking lot ahead, she smiled at her own jitters.

Soft footsteps rustled in the other direction. She spun toward the sound, and a dark figure rushed at her. *No!* In a flash, he grabbed her ponytail and jerked her toward him with a stunning force. Bettina opened her mouth to scream, but his hand clamped over it. An acrid scent burned her nose.

Oh god! He was drugging her! She reached for her mace, but dizziness overcame her. A powerful arm squeezed around her shoulders, dragging her into the trees. As her world started to go black, her last thought was, "I'm so sorry, Mama!"

Chapter 2

Tuesday, September 17, 5:45 p.m.

Detective Wade Jackson reached for his service weapon, and a terrifying scream erupted behind him. He spun around, heart pounding. The scream became a wail of agony. He started forward, then remembered the Sig Sauer holstered against his ribs. He pulled the gun, shoved it into a case on the dresser, and slammed the locking lid.

A quick sprint into the hall brought him face-to-face with the problem. Two four-year-old boys had a death grip on a plastic dinosaur toy and neither would let go. The wailing came from Micah, Kera's grandson, who was rather temperamental. But the boy had been in transition for most of his short life and had lost his mother the previous year.

"I had it first." Benjie, his adopted son, was emphatic, yet calm. He'd not only lost his mother too, he'd witnessed her murder. Yet the tragic event had given him a strange mature serenity. Jackson worried that Benjie was suppressing his anxiety, but counseling hadn't brought it out.

Jackson held out a hand. "Give it to me, please."

Benjie quickly let go, forcing Micah to be the one to hand it over. An act that made his stepbrother sob.

Kera popped out of the bathroom. "What's going on?" Tall and gorgeous, his girlfriend was always a pleasure to his weary eyes.

"Same old stuff." Jackson handed her the toy. "We need two of these."

"We have two!" Kera looked back and forth between the boys. "Where's the other one?"

Micah shrugged, and Benjie looked thoughtful. "Maybe in the toy box."

"Well, go find it. You're not getting this one back until you do." She shooed them off and leaned in to kiss Jackson. "I love it when you're home early and we can be a normal family."

Jackson laughed. "I'm not sure there's anything normal about our scenario, but I'm happy to be here too." *Sort of.* Living full-time with Kera and Micah was more challenging than he'd imagined. Having a second young child in the house generated an energy and volume he wasn't prepared for—and the more time the boys spent together, the more they fought. His daughter Katie, almost a legal adult now, had been quiet and easy as a little kid.

Jackson suppressed a sigh, followed Kera to the kitchen, and started chopping the onion she handed him. "How was your day?" he asked.

"Good." She put down the big knife she'd just picked up. "But I think I made a mistake in taking the job at the fertility clinic. It's so boring."

"You mean compared to Planned Parenthood." Jackson grinned. "I knew you would miss the chaos."

She smiled now too. "It's more about missing the variety of patients. I never knew who would be waiting in the exam room. All walks of life."

"Yeah, I get that in my job too." Jackson squeezed her arm.

"So go back to the birth control clinic. You know they'll be glad to have you."

"It pays less."

"I know. We'll be fine. You need to enjoy your work."

"Thanks for that."

"Of course."

After dinner, Jackson sat on the living-room floor with the boys, surrounded by a rainbow of blocks. They constructed a variety of towers, tearing each one down with gusto before starting another. Next they built a mutant vehicle. He yearned for one of the kids to show an interest in real cars someday. His daughter had helped him restore a '69 GTO, but she'd done it out of obligation rather than real passion, and he'd had to sell it after his divorce. They'd also built a three-wheeled vehicle he still drove sometimes. Now that he and Kera were settled into this big rental home, he was eager to get started on a new project.

When Micah got tired and cranky, Kera read a story to the boys, then Jackson helped them get ready for bed.

"Remember, tomorrow is park day." Benjie hugged him with a tight squeeze. "I love you, Daddy." The words melted his heart every time.

He and Kera changed into pajamas, got into bed to watch a movie, and fell asleep before it ended.

Jackson woke to his phone ringing. Startled and confused, he sat up, glancing at the digital clock: *12:45 a.m.* He snatched his phone from the nightstand. *Sergeant Lammers.* A strange mix of dread and adrenaline surged through him. Plus another emotion he couldn't identify.

"Is it work?" Kera mumbled, sitting up too.

He nodded, climbed out of bed, and headed into the hall for privacy. "Hey, Sarge. What have we got?"

"A dead body in the road at the corner of Greenhill and Highway 126." A pause. "I need you to take it."

"A traffic accident?" He knew better.

"No. The victim is wrapped in plastic, and a woman motorist ran over it."

What? "That's a new one."

"Indeed. That's why I called you. Besides, everyone else is already overworked."

A flash of guilt. "Do we know anything yet?"

"No. The responding patrol officer dragged the body out of the road for safety but didn't try to unwrap it."

"Good. I need to see it as is." The scene flashed in his mind. A dark roadside clusterfuck—right on the edge of city limits. "But the location is inside the boundary?"

"We're assuming so."

"Do I get a team?" The Violent Crimes Unit was overwhelmed, as always, but this time it was mostly his fault for taking medical leave for the first half of the month.

"I'll send Evans out, and we'll see what develops."

"I'm on my way." Jackson stepped back into the bedroom.

Kera was on her feet now. "A new homicide?"

"An odd one. I'll tell you what I can when I know more."

"I'll make you coffee while you get dressed."

"Thank you!" She was so good to him. He pulled on the same clothes he'd been wearing earlier and retrieved his weapon from the fingerprint safe. He hated leaving the house in the middle of the night, but at least now he didn't have to wake up his kids and take them to a sitter when it happened. He'd only had a small window of time between when his daughter was old enough to be left alone and when Benjie came into his life.

Jackson stopped, suddenly worried. *Where was Katie?* Had she come home while he was asleep? No, he would have woken at the sound. Another curfew violation. Her new boyfriend obviously didn't respect his rules.

In the kitchen, while Jackson located his travel mug, Kera said, "I used the Keurig because it's faster, but don't worry, the brew is strong."

He transferred the coffee and hugged her. "Will you try to track down Katie? I don't have the time or focus right now."

"I'll text her."

"Thanks." Jackson tried not to look, or feel, upset. "I'll probably be back around four in the morning for a couple hours of sleep."

"Are you sure you're ready for this? Your surgery was less than a month ago."

"I'm fine. Yes, the incision still hurts, but it's different. A healing pain and fading fast." The abdominal fibrosis would likely grow back again, but he refused to worry about it until it happened. "We're too short-handed for me to sit out any longer."

"And you love your work." Kera smiled.

"It's who I am." Jackson kissed her and headed out.

In the driveway, he noticed Katie's car parked on the street in front of the house. That meant her boyfriend was with her and that Aaron would likely borrow the Honda and drive it home. Jackson hated both thoughts. He jogged over, wincing at the sight of them making out in the backseat. Would he ever get used to the idea that his daughter was a sexual person?

He slapped the roof hard. "Wrap it up. Katie has a curfew!" If not for his new case, he would have hung around, making them uncomfortable.

But he was already running late. Jackson hurried to his city-issued sedan. Behind the wheel, he gunned the engine for effect as he backed out of the driveway, then stopped parallel with the other vehicle. Katie glared and rolled her eyes. Jackson pointed at the house, unsmiling. He'd accepted long ago that he had no real control over his daughter, but he maintained the right to have rules if she wanted to live in his house. Or his rental anyway. He and Kera had signed a six-month lease on this place, giving them time to look for a house to purchase. But he wasn't in any rush, and he and his brother still owned the house they'd grown up in.

As Jackson drove off, he pushed the family stuff out of his head. He had a murder victim waiting and justice to pursue.

Chapter 5

The hot-air balloon lifted off the ground, giving Agent Jamie Dallas a rush of excitement. Not exactly the adrenaline burst she experienced when skydiving or zip-lining, but still glorious—and this excursion would last longer. As the balloon drifted higher and higher, her grin widened. She loved seeing the massive city below, laid out like a grid, shrinking slowly down to a model-scale size. The wide-open blue sky drifted with clouds at eye level, and a hawk soared by.

The pilot changed directions and headed north, and soon she spotted hills, canyons, and square plots of land below. As the city faded into the distance, an eerie silence engulfed them. Even the wind quieted, and all she could hear was her own pulse.

Her heart filled with joy, and for a moment, she forgot everything else, including the other people on the flight. She loved this sensation so much. Feeling like a bird who could fly anywhere, free from restrictions or planned routes. Above and away from everything, especially the desk she'd been stuck at for a while. Away from the crime and fear and trauma she encountered on her job every day.

The excursion was an early morning birthday gift to herself, and she thought she might make it a yearly tradition. The only thing that would have made it better was sharing it with Cameron, who was in Flagstaff working. But she would see him for a late dinner tonight after he drove down. She looked forward to wrapping up this perfect day with amazing sex, a great way to say goodbye to her twenties.

Two hours later, Dallas strode into the Phoenix FBI office, feeling both at home and restless at the same time. Sliding into her desk chair, she opened her computer and scanned the bureau's news feed. Upstairs, a special team of agents and analysts stared at a roomful of monitors, watching around-the-clock for breaking events across the nation. Still, taking America's *crime pulse* was also her first responsibility. Nothing eye-popping stood out. Politics had so consumed the citizenry, that except for hate crimes, the rate of federal offenses had actually dropped.

But criminals never took breaks, so Dallas grudgingly opened a report she'd started about a local fraud ring run by a sixty-two-year-old woman with a gift for real estate scams. The grifter preyed on out-of-town seniors looking to buy winter homes in the area. Dallas had posed as a sketchy realtor to help bust the scammers. The assignment had taken her out of the office, but not out of town. And not deep enough undercover to suit her. She loved taking on a whole new persona to penetrate deep into a criminal ring. Just thinking about the risk sent a surge of juice through her body.

Her desk phone rang at the same time, startling her. Line one, her new boss. She picked up. "Good morning, sir."

"Come to my office, please. I have a high-priority assignment for you."

Yes! Dallas jumped up, adrenaline pulsing again. She hustled upstairs to the corner office where Special Agent Radner ran their division. Notepad in hand, she hurried through the open door. Behind his desk, Radner hunched forward, masking the full size of his impressive frame. His gray kinky hair, cut close to the scalp, contrasted with his dark skin tone, and his face was sweet to look at. She repressed a surge of sexual attraction and sat down. "What have you got for me?"

"An undercover job in Vancouver. A string of roofie rapes near the University of Washington campus."

"You want me to work as bait." The risk didn't bother her, but the lack of challenge did.

"You're exactly his type." Radner paused and gave her a small smile. "Blonde, blue-eyed, and attractive. You don't even have to change your looks."

Dallas nodded, trying to hide her disappointment. Like any good actress, she liked changing her appearance. That was part of the fun. So was changing her name, location, and personality. When she'd first taken acting classes in high school, she would have laughed at the idea that she would end up in law enforcement. Not with her sketchy parents. But here she was. "What do we know about the suspect?"

"Two of the earlier victims recall talking to a guy in his earlier thirties. They think he was dark blond and a little heavyset. But others, assaulted later, said he might have brownish hair but bald in front. So there could be two assailants."

"Or maybe he's changing his looks." Making her job harder. "Also, dark blonde and brownish could be the same color. And if the women were roofied, they might not remember the perp at all, maybe just the guy they talked to right before.

Agent Radner pushed a folder across the desk. "Six sexual

assault reports are in the file, plus a list of sexual predators in the Vancouver area. I've also submitted a subpoena to the university for a list of all their male students. Once we have it, our analysts will round up photos and sort the names along any demographic you ask for."

"Excellent. Who's my local contact?"

"I don't know yet, but someone will text your burner phone after you arrive in Vancouver."

"My new alias?"

"Amber Davison. Since you're not going in deep, the UC team is generating a fake ID this time. You can pick it up on your way out today."

Her excitement mounted. When she went deep undercover, she had to wait for the DMV to create a real driver's license and for the undercover team to generate background files such as school records, social media pages, and an appropriate resume. Not this time. "When do I leave?"

"As soon as you wrap up your personal obligations. You might be gone two weeks or two months. The Vancouver police haven't had any luck tracking this perp, so we know he's careful." Her boss paused for moment. "He's also escalating. The last victim woke up in his car with the engine running. She bolted but was too panicked to get a description or plate number."

"You think he was trying to kidnap her?

"Possibly."

"I'll be careful."

"And you'll wear a tracker."

"Of course." Dallas started to get up. "I'll book a flight for the morning."

"Wait. There's more."

An unexpected wave of apprehension hit her as she sat back down.

"We recently found a new group of online incels with disturbingly violent rhetoric. I need you to set up a profile and get inside. Maybe we'll spot our perp."

The assignment both excited and repulsed her. She'd read enough *involuntary celibate* rants to know how angry and irrational their attitudes were. "What's the URL?"

"It's in your folder, and the website is named Not Normal."

Dallas coughed up a harsh laugh. "No kidding. At least they have some self-awareness."

Radner shook his head. "Not really. They call everyone else—meaning those of us having sex—*normies*. But they take no responsibility for their own lack thereof. They blame women. For apparently failing to fulfill their social obligation to provide sex." Her boss looked perplexed and amused at the same time. "But you probably are aware of all this."

"I've done some reading on the topic. What else do we know about the members?"

"Their digital fingerprints come from all over the country. But some are probably tech savvy enough to use VPNs or proxy servers." Radner locked eyes with her, his long years on the job making his brow wrinkled. "There's also a lot of overlap with white supremacist organizations, so you have to assume anyone from the group is carrying."

"Got it." Dallas squirmed, eager to get started. "Anything else?"

"Don't meet anyone without backup." Agent Radner stood, signaling she should too. "Don't worry much about blowing your cover. This isn't an organized crime ring. Just a lone sexual predator."

Dallas nodded. But as she walked out, doubts set in. What if the perp didn't work alone? What if he had help and support from the group? This sting might be more dangerous than they realized.